Praise for the Books of Margaret McGaffey Fisk

Secrets

"Through her young heroine and hero, the author breathes life into a curious, exciting and often dangerous world of steam, sail, sentient machines, loyal friendships and deeds of quiet bravery undertaken in the face of widespread fear and bigotry, to deliver a clever, entertaining and unique new take on Victorian Steampunk."

— David Bridger, author of *A Flight of Thieves* (*Sky Ships*) —

Shafter

"Trina's life revolves around protecting her family and as a shafter, the lowest of Ceric society, her choices are limited to what she can steal. However, a chance at a new life aboard a colony-bound ship teaches her a new way of life and the price of unquestioned loyalty in this exciting tale, rich with cultural world building and science fiction adventure. This is a story you'll love, with a tale you won't want to see end!"

— Lazette Gifford, author of *Glory* —

"While the heroine yearns for another world, you'll crave any universe, any tale, created by this exciting new speculative fiction author. In Shafter, McGaffey Fisk delivers an interplanetary colony system and populates it with complex and sympathetic characters. Travel from the tunnels of Ceric to the stars beyond with a master thief and her master storyteller."

— Valerie Comer, author of *Majai's Fury* —

Other Works by
Margaret McGaffey Fisk

SEEDS AMONG THE STARS

(SCIENCE FICTION ADVENTURE)

Shafter

Trainee

The Captain's Chair (Indie Traders short story)

UNCOMMON LORDS AND LADIES

(SWEET REGENCY ROMANCES)

Beneath the Mask

A Country Masquerade

An Innocent Secret

THE STEAMSHIP CHRONICLES

(STEAMPUNK ADVENTURE)

Safe Haven

Secrets

Threats

Box Set 1 (Books 1-3)

SHORT STORIES (eBook only)

Forged

War Child

Curve of Her Claw (illustrated by Star Olsen)

Visit margaretmcgaffeyfisk.com for more information
about these and other titles.

Gifts

The Steamship Chronicles
Book Three

Margaret McGaffey Fisk

TTO
PUBLISHING

Cover art and design by Margaret McGaffey Fisk

Cover Photography and Text Graphics: Colin Fisk (photography) and Graechan (text graphics)

TTO Publishing logo design by Blue Harvest Creative
www.blueharvestcreative.com

Gifts

Published by
TTO Publishing

ISBN-10: 1-63139-015-5
ISBN-13: 978-1-63139-015-9

First Print Edition

Visit the author at:
Website: margaretmcgaffeyfisk.com
Twitter: @Marfisk
Google Plus: +MargaretMcGaffeyFiskAuthor
Facebook: MargaretMcGaffeyFisk

The steamship's engine ground away, taking them ever closer to the island they'd spotted at the base of the rainbow. Every member of the crew seemed to be spinning fantasies about what they'd find there, though most of them focused on the end of short rations. The ship's progress felt all too slow when clear skies and calm seas kept the island visible but out of reach.

Samantha leaned against the rail and stared at the island with the rest of the off-duty crew. They'd probably been to many islands before, unlike her, but still, relief seemed only a small part of the excitement thrumming through them.

Perhaps they saw this as an adventure after all, especially after surviving yet another fierce storm. She couldn't be the only one looking forward to solid land beneath her feet.

"You'll regret the sleep you're missing come landing," Mister Trupt said as he swept by on his way to instruct some aspect of the ship. The first mate's voice held more laughter than warning, his understanding clear.

He came to a sudden halt next to Sam. "Thanks to you for your help, especially after..." His mustache twitched when words failed him, a state she suspected came rarely.

As much to ease his discomfort as her own at being put on the spot, Sam waved off the apology. "You did nothing more than what you had to."

"And I'd do it again."

He turned and left before she could determine whether his statement came as an acceptance of hers, or a warning of what had yet to come.

She might have fixed the damaged pump so they didn't ride too low after the storm, but her knack for repairing mechanical objects came from the aether they gathered about themselves, not any training or skill. Why should the first mate trust her to control the ability when even she wasn't sure she could?

The sour thought haunted Sam as the island neared.

The charts held no mention of this one, making the likelihood of a port slim. But once they'd resupplied, the captain knew the correct heading. Soon the sailors wouldn't have to worry about a Natural wandering their decks...or transforming what powered the ship from below them.

"And would you look at that," Seamus said at her side. "You've found us a beaut of an island, Miss Samantha. So much greenery means fresh water, and like as not some game as doesn't come already doused in salt, whether salted a purpose or tugged from the salty water."

He licked his lips in anticipation, and her thoughts strayed to a fresh meal all too quickly. She'd received the same cut rations as the others when she'd been discovered, and scavenged what she could as a stowaway before that.

A little hunger and short rations were much better than the crew's first reaction, though. They'd tried to toss her overboard on a sand spit that vanished and reappeared with the tides. A death sentence.

Still, she would do much for the taste of some fruit jam like Cook prepared back at Henry's estate.

Homesickness swept over her as deep as one of the waves crashing across the deck during the previous night. Her sister and Henry would be wondering why she hadn't sent word. If only she'd found Henry's man on the dock in Dover. Then she'd be safe in a haven for people like her on the Continent instead of half a world away surrounded by rough sailors.

"You're a wonder, Miss Samantha." Hassan changed his path to stop beside her after coming down from the rigging. "A king's treasure to be sure."

Her cheeks heated at the praise, and it washed away all thought of the English countryside where she'd hidden for half her life. "I didn't do much."

His wide mouth spread in a grin as he slapped both hands on the rail and laughed. "Not much? Not much, the miracle says." The other sailors nearby joined in his laughter. "You fixed the engine 'til she's strong, you fixed the captain's crazy navigation device so he can see the earth itself, you fixed the pump so we didn't drown…" With each statement checked off on his dark fingers, the sailors let out a cheer. Then his grin became wider still as he leaned close to whisper in the carrying voice every rigger learned, "And you didn't transform our ship into a top-heavy monster."

The laughter swelled around her, and Sam appreciated the sentiment more than they could ever know. She'd never been teased about her gift instead of feared before. Not even when she'd fixed the steam-powered heater on Henry's estate. Henry's people, most of them, had accepted her as Lily's sister despite her Natural tendencies, not because of them.

Still, she heard the warning beneath the joking statement. Not so long ago, they'd expected just what he'd described from her, and they weren't all that wrong.

No matter how much hunger and desperation had kept her knack under control in the many weeks of their journey, she'd heard the engine wanting more.

Sam turned back to stare at the approaching island as Hassan wandered off, having said his piece. He'd gotten his laugh and now returned to whatever duty he'd been about when he first saw her there. It wasn't as if he could miss her, the only female in a crew of hardened sailors. She was the youngest or next to it as well.

Thought of Nat sent her scanning the crew for her friend, defender, and companion.

He'd been with her the moment she'd seen the rainbow marking their path to the island, but he'd had other tasks to see to. No one had complained when Sam stayed up top to watch their approach, but then she had sailors all around her the whole time. If she were to do anything to make them nervous, she had no doubt they'd have her bound up faster than a sail with a storm coming in.

Oddly, the idea offered some comfort.

Here, she could trust them to stop her while still being kind. Discovery had always meant imprisonment in an asylum before. Despite the respect Henry's lineage, and his own labors, commanded, there would have been dire consequences for her sister and her brother-in-law as well. The ship ran on rules as strong as any on shore, with as swift punishments, but necessity and value weighed heavier than law.

And they found value in her.

The call to assemble clanged from the bell shortly after they'd dropped anchor. It surprised no one and all of the crew had already gathered on deck.

Mister Trupt stood by the helm, the register in his hands. The list normally came out when it was time to divide up earnings, but even then it served tradition more than a true need. The first mate knew every name the sailors might have gone under, those of their own choosing and those given them.

Nat stood with the rest, no less eager to learn how he would be sent to the island. He wanted to discover whatever the lush jungle offered as much as any other despite his affection for the sea.

Mister Trupt called out the names, assigning some to hunting, others to chopping trees necessary for repairing the storm damage, and still more to seek fresh water to replenish their supplies.

Not once did Nat hear his own. Even when the first mate called out those allowed to take their leisure on the shore his name was not mentioned.

"The rest of you will be the skeleton crew. Keep the ship at ready. These are uncharted waters, and therefore hold unknown dangers, especially this close to land. Pirates or natives may pose a threat."

He snapped the register closed and turned to walk down to the captain's cabin where he would store the document.

Before he got free, the captain sprang up the short flight of steps with unexpected energy. "Mister Trupt, if you would, I need three of the men to accompany me on an exploration. This is uncharted as you've said. We will amend the charts and perhaps discover trade opportunities."

Mister Trupt scowled at the request, the ledger coming open once again as he considered his assignments.

Nat held his breath, sure this time he'd be loosed on the shore. After all, he had the most experience with Captain Paderwatch's research having kept the captain busy many a day when he'd first come aboard.

"Seamus, Pennybright, Hassan. You'll go with the captain after a visit to the armory."

Again the book snapped shut, the sound a bit more adamant the second time. Mister Trupt strode for the steps without allowing for any further interruptions.

Nat stared at the first mate, glanced at the captain, then returned his gaze to the one man with control over all shore access. Before he consciously started moving, his legs were already in motion, set on a path to intercept.

"Mister Trupt," Nat said when he'd come close enough not to shout. "Am I not to go ashore?"

The first mate's shoulders tensed. When he turned, his expression showed no significant emotion.

"Was your name called off the list?"

A flush heated his cheeks as Nat answered, "I did not hear it called."

"Then you're not to go ashore."

Mister Trupt spun and took the three strides necessary to reach the captain's cabin, but Nat could not leave well enough alone.

"But why?" he asked before rethinking the wisdom of a protest.

This time, the first mate's expression left no doubt as he glared down at Nat. "It could be because your actions have not been wholly trustworthy this voyage," Mister Trupt said, his words sharp. "It could be you sought to keep a stowaway hidden. It could be how you antagonized the engineer…"

With each statement, Nat shrank a little further, wishing his question unspoken.

"But the true reason is simple. You are responsible for Miss Samantha for all you've left her to her own devices this morning. She is to stay on board, which means so are you. Understood, Mister Bowden?"

Nat stared at the worn boards beneath his feet. "Understood."

"I did not hear you, Mister Bowden."

Nat glanced up, meeting the first mate's mild gaze firmly. "Understood, sir. I'll get on about it now, sir."

Mister Trupt relaxed both his stance and his face as he gave Nat a smile. "She's done much good and is sure to do more before we land somewhere civilized enough for her to depart. That weighs in your favor. But she is your responsibility, and fair or not, the girl has the ability to wrench the very ship from beneath us. She's not to leave your sight unless placed back in her room with the key turned. There will be no slipping on this, Mister Bowden. She will not be left to wander when so few remain aboard to monitor her."

Hearing the warning and knowing he'd been a bit too lax with the ship's rules, Nat could only nod his agreement.

"Wait here."

Mister Trupt left him to stew in his own shortcomings while the first mate entered the captain's cabin to replace the register. If not for the reputation Nat had earned since coming on board, first by keeping the captain from plaguing the crew and then by learning each part of the vessel with careful attention paid to those best skilled in the tasks, he'd have gotten more than a warning. He knew as much from when the engineer's false accusation almost ended with him hanging from the yardarm.

"Here you go, Mister Bowden. Take care not to lose this key, or our Natural. Mister Garth will be staying aboard to tend to some repairs. You are to keep out of his way and make sure Miss Samantha does the same. I will not hear of any trouble upon my return, now will I?"

Nat closed his fist around the key once used to lock him inside and now to keep the crew happy. Samantha ran free in the engine room for many weeks without causing any damage. It didn't seem fair to lock her up, especially after she'd repaired the engine and several other vital mechanical devices.

He sighed and thrust the key into his pocket. Mister Garth's story about the untrustworthy apprentice had shown well enough how expectations could be as dangerous as any reality even without his own experience with the crew's reactions.

AH, THERE YOU ARE, MISTER Bowden. I wouldn't have expected to find you already at my cabin door."

Nat turned to face the captain, half-tempted to renew his pleas to go to the island. He could bring Samantha with him, fulfilling both demands.

"Mister Trupt has much to do with preparing the equipment. We have sizable damage that I'm more comfortable patching here, with such a good supply of raw wood, than chancing a failure as we cross the wide stretch between us and the Americas. We'll be here for a number of days, I suspect, and so the crew will need a proper base on the island as well. Not to mention renewing our stores from what vegetation and meat we can find."

Captain Paderwatch got a dreamy look on his face that boded ill for Jenson. Like as not, the cook would be tasked with recreating something from the captain's extensive travels as a child and young man studying different cultures, something far apart from the simple fare the crew preferred.

"You wanted to see me?" Nat cut in before the captain got started into a tale of another voyage.

While Nat listened intently to the sailors' talk, the captain more often spoke of topics like food and marriage habits. It would be a long sail before Nat would have a use for such knowledge. Not until he succeeded in his effort to someday command a vessel himself.

The captain shook his head to clear it and narrowed his gaze to take in Nat rather than whatever he'd been contemplating from the past. "Right. Yes, Mister Bowden, I did. Step into my cabin for a moment."

Nat couldn't imagine what instruction the captain would consider so important as to delay his own explorations of the island, and the first mate had already given Nat a charge. If ever Samantha would get in trouble, this would be the time for it with the crew focused on preparations and no one paying any mind.

"Come along, Nat. I haven't much time."

"Mister Trupt—"

"Mister Trupt can wait."

Nat's shoulders curved as he gave in to the inevitable. He couldn't chance this being a true order, not when he'd stretched the captain's patience well beyond any friendship the man held for Nat's mother.

The door closed behind him with a finality that made Nat flinch. But then he'd been barred from the island. While the captain had better things to do, he must watch over Sam as the first mate commanded. He hoped she'd stay out of the way and take care.

"Mister Trupt put you in charge of Miss Samantha, did he not?"

The captain paused long enough for Nat to give an uncertain nod, surprised at the turn their conversation had taken.

"I want you to do something for the girl. I want you to transform her into the look of a boy. Cut her hair and dress her in your spares, at least until she can purchase some of her own."

"What?" Nat stared at the captain. "You can't mean what you said. She'll not stand for it. Why would you do such a thing?"

Captain Paderwatch gave a slight smile as though amused by his protest.

"She may not look it now," Nat persisted, "but you have only to talk with Miss Samantha to know she comes from a good family. She's been raised well. Why would you ask me to take away such a critical part of her being?"

The captain sank into his chair, attempting to tug it closer. He often forgot how the furniture had been nailed to the floor to prevent it from creating additional dangers in storms. The captain looked more the professor he'd been than a captain in this moment, but Nat had no patience for a lecture.

Nat braced both feet and crossed his arms to glare at the captain as much as he knew he should be practicing deference and working to win back the man's regard. "I won't do it. She's lost so much I won't take who she is from her as well."

The captain thrust a hand through the hair that clung to one side of his bare pate. "She stands out too much, Nathaniel. Every moment she's up on deck, she draws the attention of the sailors, and then they remember her nature. She saved us more than once. They know this as well as you or I do. But it takes so little to turn their regard into something darker. A miracle she might be, but her presence is tied up with luck, and luck can run bad as well as good."

He'd had the same worry often enough so Nat couldn't disagree with the statement.

Still, he planted his hands on the desk in front of the captain and demanded, "What does this have to do with stripping away who she is? We're not so large a vessel they'll be deceived into thinking her a second cabin boy you picked up before we left Dover. They know Samantha now."

The captain released a drawn out sigh and rubbed a hand across his forehead. "I've given this much thought, Nat. It's not something I suggest lightly. Miss Samantha has been an aid to us. She deserves better thanks than all I can offer her, but she cannot stay aboard. The risk is too great."

"She was with us the whole voyage and has broken nothing," Nat protested before the captain could continue.

Captain Paderwatch's eyes narrowed as he stared back at Nat. "I'm well aware of the facts. Now, at least. Had she been revealed soon out of Dover, we'd have turned back to drop her off. Instead, you saw fit to keep her presence hidden."

Nat's gaze fell first, and his fingers scraped against the wood of the desk surface. "I discovered her too far out to turn back," he said in a soft tone, not arguing so much as stating a fact. He knew well enough he should have ignored her pleas and reported Samantha to the captain when he'd first discovered her. But he hadn't known her to be a Natural then. He hadn't known his inaction put the ship at risk.

"But she didn't break anything," Nat repeated, "and she fixed some."

The heat of the captain's gaze eased a bit. Nat dared to look up only to see worry where there had been disappointment and censure before.

"The risk is not so much of a Natural on board, though I can hardly believe those words even from my own lips. The risk is more that she does not belong. She's not part of the crew, and even without her knack, her lack of place makes her vulnerable. Mister Garth still regards her with suspicion. How much would it take for the others to turn against her if something went wrong?"

The tension in Nat's shoulders made it hard to deny the charge, but he didn't see how her looks mattered. "You still plan to put her off. What difference does it make if the crew sees her as a boy? We can't be more than a week out of the Port of New York."

The captain laughed. "You need to spend less time in the engine room and more studying your charts, Mister Bowden."

He waved off Nat's attempt to remind the captain he'd been barred from the vicinity of the engine.

"The storm took us well past New York City. When we find landing in the Americas, it'll be the Port of Savannah by my calculations." He sobered. "And that is half the problem. We can't very well turn Miss Samantha over to her family when she has none in the Americas, whether New York or Savannah. The crew might not care girl or boy, but if she adopts a boy's style now, she'll have a hope of carrying it off once she disembarks. A young woman alone faces greater dangers than you can imagine, especially in a port city."

The true meaning behind the captain's request became clear, all too clear when he considered Mister Garth's charge of bringing on a doxy when Samantha was first discovered. He had only to think about the dockside women in the ports he'd seen, and the riggers' teasing, to know just what kind of life a woman without protection came to.

Captain Paderwatch nodded. "I see you get my meaning. But a boy…well, there are always boys looking for work or a berth. She'd be lost in the crowd and find making her way a sight easier without the restraints placed on the female gender."

"I understand," Nat said despite his reluctance. It did not seem fair for Samantha to give up everything just because a carriage disaster separated her from those responsible for seeing her safely to the Continent.

Now she was halfway across the world from where she'd been headed, the captain would not agree to letting her sit out the full voyage and return to England, and her safety depended on becoming what she was not. Even without her affinity to all things metal, her circumstances had sunk far below what a well-brought-up young woman could be expected to endure.

"You're a good boy—man," the captain said, breaking into his morose thoughts. "You've made many a poor decision this voyage, though you'd not be the first, nor likely the last, to have his head turned by a sweet face. It's good to see you taking responsibility for your actions. Your mother would be proud of you."

With that, he waved toward the door, clearly dismissing Nat in favor of whatever preparations the captain needed before setting out to explore the island.

Nat held the praise close, hoping he'd somehow managed to make up for those self-same poor decisions even if he couldn't quite regret most of them.

Samantha had become a friend and companion.

He might regret breaking trust with the captain, engineer, and crew, but he could not regret protecting Samantha. Nor should he with how her presence kept them safe through not one but two storms. An early departure always risked such with the winter still casting its shadow onto the spring in the form of fierce weather. Without her aid, though, they'd surely have been lost.

Nat found Samantha wandering among the piles of things collected for the shore boats. The sailors would make a camp on the beach, complete with hammocks and gear, so they wouldn't have to keep coming back and forth from the ship. Then they needed the equipment for chopping down trees, sawing up the boards, and rough sanding them, especially for the paddle replacements.

He caught up with her just as she neared the pile of armaments, rifles, pistols, and muskets, for the hunters and those responsible for the security of the camp. Unknown dangers might exist, and Mister Trupt believed in careful preparation to prevent disaster.

Nat stuck his arm through hers and subtly turned Samantha down another path towards a collection of bundled hammocks. Whether she'd been intending something or not, he didn't want to discover what she could create out of their weapons especially with him being responsible for her every action.

They ended up back on the rail where he'd seen Samantha spend most of the morning.

"What do you think they'll find over there?" she asked, pointing toward the beach where one of the shore boats had already landed.

Nat shrugged, unwilling to pretend he had any idea. "Fresh water for sure from all the growth. And some kind of meat, though it could be snake or lizard."

She turned to him, her eyes wide. "Have you eaten anything like that?"

"No, but I've heard stories from other such undiscovered islands." As much as he wished he could say yes and tell her just what it would be like, he would not boast personal experience he didn't have. And he'd only hear about this one, too, since he couldn't go ashore.

Samantha brushed his sleeve. "You want to be with them, don't you?"

Nat dropped a scowl he hadn't intended and gave her a lopsided smile. "Of course I would. Wouldn't you? It's uncharted territory. There's no telling what we'll find. It could be uninhabited, it could hold people like the captain's always talking about, or it could be a pirate haven with treasure just waiting for the taking."

She shivered, though whether with excitement or fear he couldn't tell until she said, "You really think there'll be pirates?"

He caught her hand where it still rested on his arm and gave her a gentle squeeze. "No, I don't think so. We'd have seen some sign. Pirates keep their places well protected. You don't have to worry."

Samantha slumped and her mouth pursed into a pout. "Henry had such wonderful stories about pirates in his library."

Nat laughed aloud at her statement, drawing the attention of several nearby sailors. "And here I thought you were afraid of them. I can't say I've encountered pirates myself, but from what I hear tell, they're not quite the dashing adventurers found between the covers of novels. More likely they'd slit our throats and take you captive."

Even then she didn't seem afraid, though he could see why. If they locked her up in a metal cage, she'd probably transform it into deadly armor and take out the whole pirate crew all on her own.

Somehow, when the image of her fighting the pirates formed fully, instead of being comforted, his stomach twisted.

The captain had been right about her being safer as a boy, but safer didn't mean safe. How long would she be able to hide her true nature in the confusion of a foreign port where she had no friends or family to guide her? Soon enough she would have spent all the coin on food, or worse had the purse ripped from her hands by thieves.

But what other option did she have? The captain said she couldn't stay aboard. Though the crew might welcome her now, if they changed their minds about tolerating the presence of a Natural, what could she do except be left abandoned at one port or another? Her options seemed always to return to the same one…and that with little good in it.

"Henry had a book just about perfect for this island," Samantha said, clearly unaware of how his thoughts had drifted. "I can't recall the title, but it told of a man and his friend capsized on a place much like this. They made a tree house and many great works to ease their life on the island."

Nat pushed his worries aside and stared at the lush landscape. "I know the book, I think. Robinson Crusoe, was it not?"

She turned to grin at him. "Yes. Yes, it was. Can you imagine something like that? Ending up in a place where no one else is and making it into a paradise?"

He leaned on his elbows and gazed at the jungle, his sharp eyes able to pick out what could only be fruit hanging from the branches just waiting to be snagged. "I can imagine it. Fresh fruit, fish or meat as we caught it, and never much of a worry when no one knew the island existed." He tried to remember the story his father had read to him when he'd been too young to master such a text. A laugh caught him by surprise.

"You shouldn't be so jolly about pirates if you remember the book, Samantha. He had some encounters I wouldn't wish on my worst enemy."

She tossed the hair back from her face and sighed. "True enough, but all that came before he found his island, didn't it? And you said yourself we'd have seen sign or been scared off. I wish we were allowed to go ashore and just see what it's like. Not to stay, but to visit."

"And pull down some of the fruit to fill our bellies."

Together, they leaned against the rail and sighed, but Nat had his orders, and if Mister Trupt had ever considered letting Samantha leave the ship, he had not shared the thought.

4

S am kept her gaze on the island, so close and yet not close enough when she needed something to occupy her mind. She didn't dare look at Nat until she had herself under control. Though she'd done the complicated repair on the pump only a few days before, she'd fought the aether to do so when she lacked the needed parts. Her fingers closed on the smooth wood of the rail, and she took a deep breath. The murmurs from the pile of wood and metal a short length from where they rested nibbled at the back of her mind even as she spun dreams with Nat.

His timely intervention had kept her from the weapons which, while lacking the complex gearing she'd found drew aether the most efficiently, had held onto the hopes and fears of those who carried them all too well. It took less aether when imbued with people's strong emotions, a fact she'd learned after transforming the watch that had been in Henry's family for generations. His mechanical stayed at Henry's side even though she'd been the one to give the little watch man his mobility.

A giggle escaped as she imagined a modified musket clomping behind the sailor who feared it the most. That very fear could build a strong, if unwanted, connection.

Nat gave her a strange look, and she couldn't for the life of her recall what he'd been saying just then. She shook her head, struggling for an explanation that wouldn't reveal how close she'd come to destroying the very items that would serve as their only defense if pirates should come on them in these waters.

She might have laughed at the image, but even making a weapon more efficient could eliminate its value from what Henry had told her of hunting rifles. The success of the rifle had less to do with its abilities and more to do with how those abilities were used by the hunter. Changing something as slight as the amount of pull on the trigger could throw the aim off.

"Mister Bowden," one of the sailors called, giving her a welcome reprieve. "It's not like you to be standing around when there's work to be done."

Nat flushed and tried to hide the fact with a shrug. "I'm on orders from Mister Trupt."

Both the sailor and Sam stared at him then. It took a moment before she made out his meaning.

He hadn't offered a timely intervention at random. He'd been assigned to keep her out of trouble.

"I'm the reason you're not going over there, aren't I?"

Nat put up his hands to block the question, but his expression gave him away.

"You have more important things to do, and I've had enough sunshine. I think I'd like to go lie down. Can you get the key to lock me in?"

Nat scowled at her, fists thrust against his hips. "I will not lock you in like some criminal. You're right about Mister Trupt making you my responsibility, but it's one I gratefully accept. I enjoy your company whether up here, down in the bilge, or in the engine pipes."

Sam smothered an exaggerated yawn. "I won't be much company soon. I wore myself out fixing the pump, and the storm didn't offer a comfortable rest. You have duties to see to, and I need a nap."

His eyes narrowed as he examined Sam, but the fake yawn turned into an honest one. Her words had been nothing but the truth though she'd have preferred a sun-warmed corner to the smelly dark of her chambers. She refused to hinder his position on the ship any more than her presence already had. He might have been assigned the duty of watching her, but to the other sailors he seemed to be taking his leisure while they labored.

The silence drew out until Sam thought she'd collapse under the weight of it, but before she could, Nat's shoulders slumped, losing his stern posture.

"I can't imagine you got much sleep curled on the damp floor as you were. At least your hammock's strung up and ready for use. I'll walk you down."

She bit back a sharp comment about how he didn't need to tuck her in, then realized he did. "You need to get the key." Sam didn't want to provoke his objections again, but he'd only meet his duty and free himself to aid the others by locking her in.

Nat thrust two fingers into a tight pocket sewn into his trousers and withdrew the key. "I have it already, though I see no need to lock you in. You weren't locked up when hiding in the engine room and you caused no harm."

"It's to make the crew happy," Sam said rather than admitting just how close she'd come to ending their engine and possibly the ship as well. Unlike then, now she had a full belly and the energy to act on the aether-driven desires around her. Let him think the crew needed her secured. He'd never understand her need for the same reassurance.

5

Nat helped pack the shore boats and saw them off to the island. Then he was called to assist the few remaining sailors as they began the laborious process of removing the shielding from the paddle wheels on either side of the ship. They needed to check each paddle board for signs of weakness.

When the assessment was complete, Nat worked with the signalman to report the extent of the damage to those on shore so replacements could be made from the island wood. They'd had no opportunity to repair storm damage to the paddles with the ship moving largely under steam power.

He missed the steady hum of the engine and wondered how Mister Garth faired. Once again, the engineer became the sole person allowed into the engine room. Nat couldn't blame the man as much as he regretted the loss. He'd re-enforced Mister Garth's hatred of workers drawn from the nobility when he'd only wanted to help.

"Go on then, Mister Bowden," one of the crew said, laughter audible in his tone. "We all know the reason for your distraction, and I'd guess she'll be well rested and tired of her own company by now."

The flush heating his cheeks had little to do with the crew's belief in his emotional attachment. He'd been so caught up in the repairs, and seeing what rested below the protective panels, he'd completely forgotten about Samantha and how he'd locked her below.

His failure burned as he strode to the hatch and down the steps. He'd been enjoying himself while the precious sunlight drained away until even if he brought her topside, she'd have nothing but twilight to see by. Nothing much remained to be seen in any case.

His knuckles rapped sharp on the door, perhaps too hard from the thud coming through the rough wood. He hadn't brought a lamp, the hatch still spilling down enough light to make out the space without needing to blind her, but she seemed much too clear-eyed once he pulled the door open to have been sleeping.

Still, he thought to ask as he offered her his arm, "Did you have a good rest?"

Samantha shrugged, dismissing the question in favor of, "What were you working on? I could hear such interesting sounds through the hull."

Again guilt struck him.

Though primarily composed of wood boards, the paddles would most likely have been just as exciting for Samantha to see, maybe more so after her close study of the steam engine. A complicated set of gears driven by the engine allowed each wheel to turn independently at the steersman's command. The elegant design would amaze even someone with no interest in machinery.

"I could show you, though the light's fading so quickly soon they'll be nothing but shapes in the dark."

"My eyes are well adjusted to the dark," she said with a laugh. "It's you who will have trouble seeing."

Her statement proved his suspicions true. If she had napped at all, it had been for a short time alone. "Why didn't you light your lamp?"

Samantha paused as she started up the steps. "I supposed I didn't think it necessary. I have nothing much to see in there, and lamp oil is unlikely to be found hanging from a tree."

Nat cursed under his breath at her easy answer. He didn't deserve what could only be a kindness when she'd earned the right to her complaints.

"Sven's serving out the stew Jenson left for us," a voice called as they came up on deck. Nat couldn't see a face to match to it, but waved in the general direction. "We'll be along shortly."

A quiet chuckle came in reply, but think what they might, he'd promised Samantha a look at the bared paddle wheel. If he had any sense of when the moon would rise, he'd time their trip then. The twilight hindered his vision enough to make his steps hesitant.

The same could not be said for Samantha. She tugged his arm to speed him as she moved not to the rail they'd been leaning on in the morning but to the other side where the wall of her prison rested.

"Why it's like a mill," she cried, leaning much too far over the edge for his comfort. "So that's what the steam engine powers through its pipes."

Nat put a hand on her shoulder to make sure she wouldn't tip over. "The steam powers gears, more even than you've seen since some rest within the walls themselves. Those gears force the wheels around, and the paddle boards push against the water to drive us forward."

She glanced at him, head tipped to one side. "Not much like the mill paddles at all then, are they? Backwards even. Where the water drives those wheels these drive the water."

He shrugged. "I haven't had much chance to see a mill, nor the paddle wheels before today. They rest below thick panels on all but the lowest point. Otherwise we'd have to stow the wheels when the weather gets rough as earlier ships did."

"Seems a waste to keep them locked up when you need the push the most."

Samantha didn't appear to notice the parallel between her own situation and those early steam wheels. Naturals, even her, were kept locked away when who knew what she could do to help if given the chance.

He stared out across the waters, blind to all but the flickering reflections of stars against waves.

The problem with Naturals lay in that very conundrum. No one knew and none were willing to take the risk. They had cause enough for the caution from the tales he'd heard told, but he'd never heard of anything like the way Samantha could choose to repair over a change, or how she could stay focused much like a skilled craftsman. If industry leaders were to learn of her abilities, she'd be snatched up faster than he could blink.

A shiver ran up Nat's spine at the thought.

They'd keep her secured just as much, or more so because none would be given the task to guard her up on deck as he had. They'd have no cause to allow her any freedom at all.

"You make sure she doesn't touch anything, boy," Mister Garth ground out on his way to the bow with his bowl.

Nat stared after the engineer. That man, of any of them, should have been the first to recognize her value. Instead, he refused to consider the possibility.

Samantha laid a hand on his arm, startling him. "Don't worry," she said. "I wasn't going to touch anything."

"I never thought you were." Nat forced a smile. "Can you see the spring-hinges? They keep the paddles stiff but not stiff enough to break if something bumps them."

Samantha leaned over the side and squinted, clearly fascinated.

Nat wished he could say the same, but the engineer's dislike only added to his worries, not eased them. What if the man saw fit to spread the word once they dropped Samantha at the port? Who would ever know? Certainly not the captain.

6

Nat had spoken truthfully when he'd told Sam about the poor lighting, and with no sign of the moon, soon she could make out nothing of significance either. But he stood lost in thought, and she couldn't bring herself to break the moment.

She'd had little to do beyond thinking while the heat of the day eased, though the water-logged air made it hard to tell when night began to fall without other clues. At least up here, she had a faint breeze to push the moist air about.

Her hands itched for something to explore, her mind just as eager, but nothing lay in reach. While supper might offer a distraction, she had little need for food what with the rich breakfast Jenson had put together in anticipation of renewing his stores with fresh once they went ashore.

Nat moved all of a sudden, startling a squeak out of her as he grabbed hold of her hand. "Samantha, we could go to the island. We could live like Robinson Crusoe and Friday."

His voice came out in an urgent whisper, but Sam laughed. "Which of us do you see as the servant?" She shook her head before he could reply. "That is nothing but a fanciful dream, Nat. You know as well as I do nothing waits for us on some uncharted island in the middle of the ocean. You have plans. You've told me of them often enough. You can't make captain of even the smallest ship when trapped on an island."

He caught her face between his palms, his body close enough she could feel the puff of each breath he exhaled. "And what of your plans? You think it will be easy stepping off the ship into an unknown port? You think to blend right in with your fancy words and odd thoughts? What of when you slip. When they find out what you can do?"

Sam pulled back, no more eager to consider her prospects than she'd been in the afternoon when she had nothing else to ponder. "Maybe Naturals aren't treated the same way in the Americas."

"You think our crew has never seen the Americas? They come from all over, and ended up sticking with Captain Paderwatch just because he turns the least worthy passage into a profitable one. I've listened to their tales for a couple of years now. Never once have I heard of a Natural working happily alongside others. Every tale—every single one—is about how something went wrong, profits and even lives were lost. Why do you suppose no crew has ever come in with a tale like ours? Why do you think the crew expects many a free round of drinks before their listeners laugh them aside for having such a fine grasp on the imagination?"

"How should I know? My experience on board has largely been spent tucked in one corner or another with only the rhythms of speech to entertain me beyond the engine's song. They come through the walls without words to inform."

He caught her again, this time by the shoulders, and held too firm for her to pull away. "And that's exactly what you'll face out there in the so-called civilized world. England, the Americas, or even on the Continent you so hoped to reach."

Nat's fingers tensed. "Just how long do you think you'll be able to hide with no family or friends to protect you? How long before someone figures you out? Don't think I haven't noticed how your fingers twitch even now for something to pull apart or bring back together. How long would you remain undetected? And once you are found out, I swear to you, there's worse than the ship's bilge to be cast into. It's foul, but has an honest nature to it. Not so where others would put you."

Sam opened her mouth to explain about the haven Henry had found for her then shut it, the words unspoken. The haven she'd been seeking existed half a world away, and the route to it had vanished along with everyone who'd intended to help her. She had no reason to believe there would be something similar in the Americas, and even less cause to believe she'd be able to find it on her own. But though she'd mulled over her choices thoroughly, she had no better option. She could not stay on board. She'd promised the captain, and the crew went along with his decision to keep her because she'd be gone in a short time. She could not have Nat putting himself any further at risk than he already had.

"You see? There's no argument to be made. The best option, the only option I can see, is to make landing here, on this island."

She failed to keep the bitterness from her tone as she snapped, "You'd abandon me here so much easier than among strangers? At least then I'd have the chance at a job and a roof over my head. Here, I'd have nothing. No tools, no skills, and no one to talk to."

He pressed a finger to her lips, making Sam aware just how loudly she'd spoken.

"You wouldn't be alone. I'd come with you. And the crew is making a basic settlement already. We'd have shelters to choose between, a cook house, and more. We'd make it work."

She stared at him, the moon having finally made its appearance to reveal his earnest features. "I couldn't. You didn't ask me to come here. You shouldered the burden, risking your reputation not once but many times on my behalf. I couldn't take everything you've worked so hard for from you as well."

His lips curved into a smile, and she swore his eyes shone by more than the reflected moonlight. "You wouldn't be taking. I am giving this to you. It's a sacrifice I make willingly for the pleasure of your company, and for the assurance you wouldn't end up locked in a dank room surrounded by the insane."

She reached up to press her palm against his warm cheek. "You're a good friend, Nat. I'm glad to have known you. But I cannot do this thing. Even if I were willing, I cannot swim. The distance between here and the shore would mean my death."

Just then, the slap of bare feet reached them and Sam turned to see the sailor called Sven approaching with two steaming bowls.

"I'm not Jenson to keep the fire going and feed the whole crew. You'd best eat now, or it'll be cold."

From his grin, he'd hoped to catch an earful, but Sam could tell they'd kept their words quiet enough. Still, she was grateful the uncomfortable conversation had ended.

Sam took the bowl and followed the sailor back, Nat at her side. At least now she could sit with them to hear their stories first hand, though she suspected they'd refrain from any involving out-of-control Naturals, whether for her sensibility or their own comfort she didn't know.

Nat rose the next morning with the sun's first rays, determined to follow the captain's orders to the letter. He'd tried to turn Samantha from this path and failed. Instead, he'd do whatever possible to help her succeed.

He dug through his chest in search of clothes he'd outgrown, sure he could find something. His parents' pre-industry wealth meant he had spares when most sailors were lucky to have a second shirt.

Sam's bones lay thicker than his, but his mother had chosen loose clothes so he could have room to grow, knowing he'd have little chance to replace the clothing at sea. Only in this last year had some of his trousers become so short as to resemble a child's clothing, an impression Nat had been desperate not to allow. He'd shoved them to the far corner of his chest.

Shirts proved more difficult as those he'd planned to discard had largely been torn up for bandages already. Besides, they had grown too threadbare to offer much of a disguise. Even worse, like her skirt, the material making them up would cause her to stand out as much as being female. Sailors did not take too kindly to the lordlings cast among them.

Nat chose the best two for on the ship, but she'd have to purchase new ones when they made port.

Some time had passed before he arrived at her door, but Samantha still did not respond to his knock at first. He tried to knock louder despite how the cloth in his arms muffled the force as much as his effort not to spill the lamp oil.

"Samantha. It's me. Nat. I'm opening the door."

His statement prompted a squeal and a scrambling noise he just might have mistaken for rats weeks earlier.

Trying to school his grin, Nat waited before turning the key. But his lips firmed when he remembered the task ahead, all humor draining from him. A squeal like she'd just made would give Sam away to the first sailor encountering the awkward boy, only one more habit he needed to strip from her.

"I'm ready," she said all too soon after his realization.

When he swung the door wide to see her still smoothing the fabric of her skirt, his expression couldn't have been less than grim.

She glanced from his face to the bundle of cloth in his hands, her forehead furrowed. "It's frayed a bit on the edges, but surely my skirt does well enough. It's not like the sailors want me climbing the rigging after them."

Instead of the chuckle she'd clearly been trying to provoke, Nat shook his head as he crossed to set the lantern down on her table. Then he dropped the two sets of clothing into her hammock.

"You may end up climbing rigging after all, though I wouldn't recommend such work."

She stared at him in silence for long enough to make him want to squirm.

"Are you cross with me still?" Sam said at last. "You must see your idea no less than madness. No one will sign a girl to a ship on purpose. At least not to work."

Nat shrugged. "I thought so at first, too, but the captain's behind this plan, and he's got the right of it. I don't think leaving you to find your way at a strange port sits any better on his conscience than mine."

"His plan is to make me one of the sailors? Nat, they know what I am and are none too comfortable with it most times. How can I hope to win their regard when I stand against so many fears? You, yourself, told me about the tales. The only answer is to leave when we reach a port. Can you not accept this truth and stop badgering me about it?"

Her voice rose on the last, and her eyes flashed with anger, the expression much like how she'd appeared when the aether demanded she repair the broken pump and madness overtook her.

Nat stared, dumbstruck by her demand.

Sure, he'd argued with Captain Paderwatch at first, but she seemed determined to reject any plan with a chance of success, no matter how slim. Did she think to step off the ship, find a job, and lose herself in obscurity?

He'd thought she had experience in the bigger world from how well she'd managed so far, but now he had greater sympathy with the sailors who'd suffered his book learning. Clearly she'd crafted her future from between the pages of novels.

"It's better you accept the truth," Samantha said, breaking into his thoughts. "Just think how much more I'd stand out as a girl in trousers than just a girl."

A laugh came strangled from his throat despite his worries. He slapped a palm to his forehead as punishment for forgetting the most important part of the captain's plan.

She peered at him as if thinking he'd gone insane, and to her eyes, maybe he had.

Nat struggled to gain control of his humor, but her pinched features made the transition to a sober nature so much more difficult.

"You'll not be a girl," he finally managed between gasps for air. "The captain's plan is you'll go as a boy."

She sank to the floor, hands twisted in her skirts. "A boy? But I've worked so long at learning to be a lady."

Nat folded his legs under him to sit at her side. "I know it's hard to give up who you have been, but the risks as a boy are so much less when you're on your own. Trust me in this."

Samantha gave him an odd look he couldn't quite interpret then pushed to her feet. "Turn your back. I'll see if the clothes you brought me fit."

He'd fought the captain longer on her behalf than this, and his little sister would have been in tears, but she barely waited for him to face the door before he heard the rustle of cloth. Nat shook his head as he stared fixedly at the door. Had she always been like this? Were all Naturals so quick to change like their mechanical objects or was it just Samantha?

A short time later, shorter than he'd have thought possible with his sister as a judge, she said, "You can look now."

He rose and turned all in one movement, ready for just how much work remained to make her passable.

Again, a laugh burst from him unexpected as he stared. "You could easily be mistaken for a boy." A flush burned his ears as he realized what he'd said, but she didn't seem to notice as she stood there, one fist on a hip and her shoulders thrown back.

She was like no female he'd ever known.

His consternation must have been visible on his face as she started laughing as well. Her long red locks fell around her shoulders and glinted in the lantern light.

"Now you look more like Samantha," he said, the clothes making less of a difference with her hair loose and her stance more normal. He shouldn't have found the fact as comforting as he did.

She frowned where any other girl would have been relieved. "You refused to call me Sam when I first told you my name, but you'll never see me as a boy if you persist in calling me Samantha."

He bit back the thought he'd never see her living as a boy anyway. The captain trusted him to help her survive once they left her, and he couldn't do so still thinking her a girl. "You're right, Sam. It's just hard to see you that way even now."

She tilted her head to one side to examine him, and before he could figure out what she was up to, she'd mimicked a posture so familiar he could recognize it on her form. "It's easier to learn to be a boy than it ever was to be a girl. Lily would be so disappointed."

"Your sister would be happy to know you safe, whatever we have to do to make it come about."

She smiled then, accepting his comfort, or so he thought until she added, "You mistake my meaning. My sister spent endless hours trying to turn her wild child into a proper lady. The state of my toes rarely spoke of her success."

As a one, they glanced down at the bare feet poking from trousers that hung a bit past her ankles.

Nat pressed his lips together. "I haven't shoes to fit you."

One foot wrapped around the other leg as if in an attempt to hide its naked state, but standing, she couldn't conceal both. "I don't need shoes. You and the rest go barefoot most of the time, and the boots Lily made me wear are hardly what a simple boy would possess."

As much as he wanted to disagree, Nat could not. "You'll need shoes if you want to get a job in a true shop, though there's places dockside you could get away with your toes visible as long as your calluses are up to the task."

She bent to fold back the cuffs, making him realize she'd avoided doing so in the first place to hide her feet. This, more than anything, proved the hint of many scoldings must be the truth.

"My calluses are as sturdy as any much to my sister's despair."

"Which leaves only one more piece."

His grim pronouncement got her full attention, but she showed no sign of comprehension on her face.

He pulled his knife free with one hand, and procured a simple ribbon from his pocket with the other. "Your hair is much too long, even confined, to pass for a boy's. And how it hangs around your face makes you look more the girl than a girlish boy as well. It'll have to go."

For the first time in this whole process, she looked startled. Samantha caught a fistful of hair and held it up to the light. "All of it? As short as yours?"

Nat waved the ribbon. "I brought this so you can tie it back in a queue. I wear mine off the back of my neck, but I fear you'd burn too quickly with nothing as a protection."

He stepped back to look her over. "As long as you keep it raked back, with the clothes and a boy's stance, you should pass well enough." Nat kept his eyes averted from her chest as he added, "Until you grow more, that is. You'd best have come up with a stronger solution by then, though of what I cannot imagine."

"If I'm frugal and careful, I'll have earned enough to buy passage to the Continent before it's much of an issue, faster now as a boy than perhaps I could have as a girl."

She seemed so confident Nat let himself believe she had a chance at this.

Still, when he stepped closer, knife in hand, she shrank away first before laughingly correcting her position so he could hack at her thick curls.

"You'll have a hard time keeping these confined, but there's nothing for it. Enough Scots and Irish around about most ports that such curls on a boy should pass unnoticed, especially in the colonies from what I hear."

Samantha made no response beyond the occasional yelp when he pulled too hard as he sliced her hair to rest just above her shoulders. He picked the ribbon up from where he'd laid it on her hammock and tied the locks back into a tight queue, at the point of the ribbon at least. From there it sprung into an uncontrolled bundle, enough to protect her neck from the sun's rays if not as elegant as he'd been trying for.

"Are you done, then?"

He stepped around her, stopping to examine Samantha from every angle. "I'm done. You'll pass at a distance, though whether any will be convinced up close depends on you."

"I wish I had a mirror," she said, running her fingers over the queue. Her hands dropped back down to her waist suddenly as if expecting a longer resistance.

Nat shook his head. "That's one thing you'll have to forget about. You'd do better to keep some dirt on your face, and your hair uncombed."

Samantha threw back her head in a delighted laugh. "I didn't want to check a mirror to admire my looks," she said, shoving him hard in the shoulder. "I merely wanted to see how I now appear. It's not like I've had a comb to tend my curls anyway. Lily would have attacked them with a scissor, but the end would be much the same."

He mimicked how she tipped her head as he pretended to contemplate her new appearance once again. "You look fully the wild child."

She growled and swatted at him, but he ducked, reaching the door only to toss back over his shoulder, "You'll need to work on your voice and your limp hands if you're to pass as a boy."

He regretted the tease a moment later when she landed a solid punch on his shoulder hard enough to shove him through the doorway and leave a throbbing bruise.

"Enough. You punch like a boy for sure, and I've no cause to fight with you. I'd prefer to see if Sven needs a hand getting breakfast."

8

S am chased him out of the room and up the steps, bursting onto the deck full of laughter at his mock terror. Lily might have spent many an hour teaching her how to be a lady, but Henry liked to swing her about and wrestle when her sister wasn't around.

She stumbled, her heart twisting to think she might never see them again. Without her laughter, she became aware of an odd stillness to the ship.

Even locked in her room, she'd been aware of working noises and the rumble of voices. But now the air hung silent like the inhaled breath of wind before a storm.

A quick glance about showed Nat with his face reddened well past his ears and a handful of sailors all staring at her with eyes wide. As if of one mind, they turned aside, some coughing, others just getting about their work with sudden urgency.

Where she'd felt full of confidence below with Nat as witness, now Sam became aware of how her borrowed trousers lay close to her skin and no layers of cloth surrounded them. She hadn't even enough cloth to twist through her hands. She found a pocket to thrust one into, but somehow her palm pressed tight to her thigh seemed worse.

"Captain's orders," Nat announced to no one in particular, using the projecting voice he claimed came from being up on the ropes.

The sailors looked back then, and one after the other came to gather before them.

"Captain thought she'd do well as a boy?"

"Needed someone to school with you proven worthless, eh, Nat?"

"Can't say as it's much of an improvement."

Sam hung behind Nat, overwhelmed by the attention and curiosity.

"Can't you see you're scaring her," Nat scolded.

"Doesn't make much of a boy cowering behind you," one of the men said.

She couldn't tell if the sailor meant to tease or was just being mean, but Sam was never one to let a challenge stand. If she had been, her sister's lady's maid would have had her in tears more often than not.

Straightening her shoulders, she stepped around Nat. "I'm not afraid of the likes of you," she said with every ounce of confidence she could muster.

"Boo!"

She jumped straight into the air as one of the sailors off to the side shouted the scare.

The others all laughed and laughed, some falling to the deck, and rolling back and forth.

She stamped her foot and thrust both fists onto her hips much like Henry's cook would do when annoyed. "I'm glad to be such entertainment," she said, putting as much strength behind her voice as she'd heard Nat do. She might never have the chance to run the ropes, but she knew how to mimic well enough.

The laughter died, not all at once, but slowly, the sailors having the courtesy to look a bit ashamed. But when they crossed her gaze, they were like as not to start off again with smothered chuckles.

After the third time, Sam failed to keep up her offended stance as a giggle escaped her lips as well.

"You all having too much fun for grub?" Sven asked, stomping up from the galley. "Here I thought you'd be starving."

His rant broke off at the sight of the sailors, many of whom were still on their backs. Then his glance swept over Sam, and his mouth fell open but nothing issued forth.

Sam gave him a shy smile. After all, he hadn't laughed at the sight of her.

"We, Nat and I that is, were coming to offer a hand with breakfast."

He looked her up and down. "Now if that don't beat just about anything. You weren't much of a girl before, no offense, but I think the captain's gonna catch on to a new cabin boy."

She laughed and shook her head all at once, surprised when her hair didn't come forward to hide her burning cheeks.

Nat stepped around her. "It's the captain's idea. She can't stay on board, but he wasn't happy about dumping her at a port with no one to go to. At least as a boy, Samantha will have a chance."

"Sam," she said, her tone firm. "And if I'm to find work as a boy, I'd best start learning, don't you think?" She looked not at Nat but to Sven.

He processed this information and shrugged. "I don't see why not. There's nothing in the kitchen to draw your special attention—at least nothing Jenson will care about—and I can sure find something for idle hands. Done enough stints with

Jenson myself so's I got elected cook with him off on the island. Is not a task down there I don't have a grasp of."

She followed him to the galley and Nat trailed after. More of the others than should have found an excuse to poke their heads in while she peeled potatoes to thicken the midday stew and Nat scraped the scales from some fish caught just this morning. The porridge for breakfast bubbled and popped over the fire with Sven giving it the occasional stir.

"I wouldn't have thought a girl like yourself would want to go to a wild island like this one," Sven said when she expressed a desire to see the new land.

Sam glanced down at the shirt she wore. "I don't expect you've met many girls like me."

He looked toward a machine up on the shelf across from her, one that had drawn her gaze a time or two though she did not recognize its purpose nor did the mechanism have enough aether to tell her. "I'd have to say none. I've met nary a one like you, Miss Samantha, girl or boy."

She ducked her head. "It's just Sam now. For me, you, and everyone. I've always preferred Sam."

The machine caught her gaze again, but this time she saw what sat in a glass jar beside it. "That's just the thing to make your meal tasty," she said, surging toward the container without thinking.

Nat leapt up to bar her way just as Sven caught her arm in a tight grip.

Sam stepped back, her gaze on the wood beneath her toes. "I only meant to get the spice," she said, her voice soft and hesitant.

Nat returned to his stool, and Sven dropped his hold to peer at the shelf. "You mean this?" he asked, picking up the jar and rattling the sticks of cinnamon within.

Nodding as she glanced up to see what he held, Sam added, "Cook says it's what makes her porridge so grand."

He shook the jar again, his brows lowering. "Sticks?"

"Spice. Cinnamon."

Sven stared at the jar. "Don't have much call for fancy stuff like that unless it's at the captain's table, I suppose."

She rubbed her arm and reached for the small knife she'd been using to shave the potatoes. "It doesn't matter."

With a grunt, Sven nodded toward her arm. "Sorry for that, Miss Samantha. I thought…"

She shook off both the apology and the guilt prompting it. "I should have asked first. And it's Sam."

His thick eyebrows rose and his mouth crinkled into a smile. "Sam then. It seems to me, Sam, from the dust on this bottle, Jenson has little need of it. I can toss a stick or two in if you'd like."

She bounced up again, but neither Nat nor Sven reacted poorly. "You don't need a full stick, not for so little. Just a sharp knife."

The others leaned close to watch when she shaved some of the cinnamon stick into the porridge, and both breathed deep as the wet steam made the smell come alive.

Sam had not realized how much she'd absorbed when spending her hours in the kitchen, but of all of Henry's staff, Cook had been her one true friend. Cook cared less for her dangerous talent and more for the way she savored the food, and consumed great quantities of it as well.

As though on cue, her stomach gave a loud rumble.

"I'm guessing you now think it smells like something worth eating," Sven said, the teasing clear this time.

"It sure does to me," Nat added.

Sven swept the big pot off the fire and nodded toward the pile of bowls. "Seems we should bring it up on deck and serve the crew then."

Sam copied Nat in rubbing her dirty hands on a scrap of cloth left out for the purpose before grabbing half the bowls. She only hoped the cinnamon was enough to cover the scent of fish sure to linger on Nat's palms.

9

Nat wondered if Sven had vouched for Samantha as the sailors emptied their porridge bowls after including her in the usual teasing. Only Mister Garth stayed separate, sending a glare in their direction as he headed off to his solitude.

She didn't even flinch, or maybe didn't notice, as Sven described the twigs she'd convinced him to add to their meal in great detail.

Perhaps the reason for their welcome could be found in the very same aromatic meal. All of them benefitted from her grand idea to grate a little cinnamon over the boiled grains.

Jenson wasn't inclined to use the spices the captain had ordered brought aboard, but Nat was surprised by how much flavor such a little bit could offer. He'd never seen his mother's staff prepare the meals and assumed a much more complicated process.

"You've won them over through their stomachs," Nat said. "Most respected of the crew members beyond the captain and first mate has got to be the cook. No one goes about offending the man."

She ducked her chin and stared at the deck, her odd reaction making his words catch up to him. A flush heated his neck.

"I didn't mean it that way. I just meant the porridge sure tastes good, and it's all your doing. Sven's sat a time or two for

Jenson. They know better than to believe the improvement came at his hand even if he hadn't spread the word as he did."

She rubbed her bare toe against a place where the deck boards had worn smooth. "Are you sure Jenson won't be offended. I mean, if Sven wouldn't have used the cinnamon, Jenson is likely to expect it still there."

"You heard him about the layer of dust. Don't worry so much. I swear to you Jenson will not miss it. He hates spices beyond the salt to preserve things and a good shake of pepper."

He glanced up from his bowl when she didn't respond to find her giving him an odd look. Only then did he realize what he'd said.

Nat gave an exaggerated peer around as though checking the first mate hadn't snuck back on board to catch him out.

"You shouldn't use your word so lightly," she said with a chuckle.

"I don't know how you came to hear him, but he sure says it often enough."

She shrugged. "Some voices carry through the engine pipes better than others, even when used softly."

"That they do." Nat remembered all too well how they'd heard Mister Garth clearly when tying off loose pipes during a storm and had prayed he couldn't do the same. If he had, Samantha would have been discovered much sooner.

"So..." She put her empty bowl to one side. "What should we do next?"

"A good question," Sven said, coming up beside them. "I'm thinking you might just haul up some water and wash out the dishes."

Nat groaned.

"And you still have fish to scale," Sven told him. "There's tasks a plenty you can undertake as easily with four hands as two."

She looked at the sailor with gratitude, her expression making the worst kitchen tasks into some kind of a boon. But then, she probably thought he'd take her back down and lock her in for the rest of the day. Even scrubbing burnt porridge out of the heavy black pot would seem better as it meant being up on deck.

"We just need to find you some shade, Samantha—Sam." He stumbled over the name that didn't suit his image of her. "Otherwise you'll burn something awful."

"You should let her burn," Sven cut in, frowning. "No one will believe she's come off a stint as a cabin boy with her soft skin. You want her to be a boy, she's got to take the same wear and tear."

Nat knew the sailor spoke the truth, but he remembered his first week on board, how his scholarly pallor crisped into hard sores when it didn't crack and peel. The sailor's remedy of fish oil hadn't been much better. He'd been plagued with nightmares of falling overboard and being gobbled up by an enterprising shark that would never know it had eaten something different than its normal fishy fare.

As if his wishes had no weight, Sam gave the big sailor a grin. "I promise to get as much sun as I'm allowed," she told Sven. "Though you'll find I don't turn color much at all. I've always preferred the open sky to the parlor."

The sailor shook his head, but not to argue as he smiled back at her. "You are sure a strange one, Sam, but in this, it'll help you."

10

hrough unanimous decision, if she didn't count the engineer, the skeleton crew declared she'd take over Sven's tasks as cook, freeing him to other duties. Nat might have grumbled at first since it meant he was locked into the kitchen chores with her, but he soon regained his good humor, especially when the others agreed to parcel out the cleaning up between them.

"I'd hoped to get a closer look at the paddle wheels," he said as they headed to the galley.

Sam nodded her agreement, but better this than locked in the bilge room. "I'm sorry everyone liked the porridge so much."

He laughed, shaking his head. "Don't be sorry. I enjoyed it as much as any of them. I think Jenson is going to take advantage of at least one spice when he hears about this. Never a better boat than one filled with full bellies."

She followed after him, even copying the jump that sailed her over four steps to land a bit unsteadily at the bottom of the stairs.

Nat caught her arm, balancing Sam until she could stand on her own.

Sam thanked him with a smile, but it quickly turned into a scowl once she found herself again in the kitchen.

"I thought you wanted this," Nat said with a wave to indicate the room.

"I did." She lifted both shoulders in a shrug. "I just didn't think it through. The trick with the cinnamon, well, I learned it from sitting in the kitchen watching Cook. They'll be expecting something for midday, and I haven't the least idea of how to get started."

"Figures they wouldn't think to ask if you could cook before foisting the task off on us. Good thing I've spent more than a few hours helping Jenson myself. Come on. We'll get a stew going with the fish I've been scaling and those potatoes you peeled. While it bubbles, maybe we can sneak up to check out those paddle wheels. It's not often the paneling comes off. Like the engine, they're rare enough to have special carpenters in charge when we land at a port. If Mister Garth hadn't complained of pulling against the gears, I doubt we'd be working on them even now after the pummeling from two storms."

The fish stew came together much faster than Sam had expected. They had few ingredients on hand, and Nat knew more than possibly even he suspected. It helped how he regaled her with tales of his two years aboard this ship and the cast of characters filling its berths.

"You'd never guess it from the look of her, or from their grumbling, but every one of us has had the choice of another crew a time or two. Mister Trupt runs a tight ship, and we've had unconscionable luck. Heck, some might even say you're a part of the bounty, coming as you did out of nowhere just when our engine had been at its absolute worst. Since you had a hand in repairing it, we've been on steam more than sail. That's the first time I can say so since I joined Captain Paderwatch's crew."

Sam's cheeks heated at the compliment, but she just ducked her head and kept working. It didn't matter how well they thought of her now. The captain had made it clear she had no place on this ship, and she couldn't blame him. He only guessed what she knew to be absolute truth. Given the right circumstances, and an aether-driven bout, she'd be like as not to transform their lucky vessel into a weight no amount of wood could keep afloat.

"There," Nat said, startling her out of her sour thoughts. "I think it's best we leave it be. Unless you know of some grand mix of powders to make ambrosia from fish stew."

Glancing around the galley, Sam saw nothing that triggered a specific thought. She picked up the pepper pot, which had not a speck of dust on it unlike the cinnamon. "Toss in a pinch of good black pepper and we should be fine," she said, mimicking Cook.

He gave her an odd, sideways glance, but then he wouldn't recognize the voice she used. He did not, she noticed, ignore the advice though it came second hand.

"Should we put some more wood on the fire?"

Nat laughed. "Not if we plan to leave it unattended. We'll have to come back and check, but for now, it should be fine."

He caught her hand and pulled her toward the door. They scrambled up the steps to the deck from where they could hear all sorts of interesting bangings and hammerings.

They pushed through the hatch together, laughing, only to come to a halt as they took in the collection of sailors now on board, including a stern Mister Trupt.

"Been wasting your time down in the hammocks, Mister Bowden?"

Nat turned a brighter shade of red than she'd ever seen on him before, and he dropped her hand as though she, not he, were covered in fish oil. "We were making the midday," he managed with hardly a stammer. "Fish stew from what some of the men caught this morning."

Mister Trupt's thick eyebrows rose high on his domed forehead. "Did you make enough for the lot of us?"

Sam watched the tension drain from Nat's shoulders at the simple question without a reprimand.

"It's the girl who's in charge," Sven called from where he was helping shift the first load of strange fruits and vegetables the sailors had collected. "Should have seen what she did with our breakfast."

If anything, the first mate's eyebrows rose even higher, and Sam felt a blush heat her face just as it had Nat's moments ago. "I only added cinnamon, Mister Trupt, sir," she said as politely as she could manage.

He shook his head, but a smile twitched both sides of his mustache. "Sweetening them up, are you? No wonder I've gotten such good reports about your assistance. And with Bowden keeping an eye on you, I reckon the galley's much the same? No self-motivating pots or knives taken to peeling all on their own?"

Though he seemed to be teasing, Sam dropped her gaze to the boards, twisting one toe against a rough spot. "I didn't touch anything to change it," she muttered to the wood grain.

Out of the corner of her eye, she saw him glance to Nat for confirmation which he must have received since he nodded once. "Seems to me you've both been doing your best for the crew and the ship. Those as have shared the space with you think so as well." He looked to Nat again. "You even turned the key in the lock from what I gather."

Nat straightened and Sam did also.

"I followed my orders."

Mister Trupt grew silent then, staring at Sam as if he'd never seen her before. "So it seems, Mister Bowden. So it seems."

Only then did Sam remember her clothing. One hand wandered up to tug on her bound hair. Unlike the sailors, the first mate didn't seem the least put out by her change. Judging from his comment, he may have known the captain's plan before she did.

"Those trousers should serve you a sight better than your skirts on the island. No paved roads there, and we've cut just a few passages."

She stared at him, her mouth falling open on a protest she didn't dare voice. He meant to leave her here with no one to talk to ever.

This time his expressive eyebrows lowered into a frown as he took in her widened eyes. "The men had given me the impression you'd enjoy a stroll through the wilderness. Thought it somewhat amusing coming from a girl. Were they mistaken?"

Sam scrambled to process his words, her fears falling to the wayside. "You mean for me to go exploring? To see the island?"

Whatever the confusion before, he seemed to understand her eagerness all too well now. "What else would I have meant? I already know Mister Bowden would give his left pinky for the opportunity. His responsibilities to you were all to hold him back. With your new appearance, and the will to see this uncivilized land, I see no harm in letting you have the same chance as the others left to keep the boat. If it pleases you?"

He ended the last with a question, and she had to restrain the desire to hug him tight as she would have Henry when offered such a prize.

"Yes. Yes, it pleases me. I desire to discover this place for myself. I've never been anywhere like it."

Mister Trupt laughed then and brought Nat into the conversation with a sweep of his hand. "I don't imagine you have. Either of you. This is not some tended garden ones like you wander in London for the pleasure. You'll stay with the others, and Nat, you'll keep your knife handy. We don't know what kinds of dangers linger here. If you get yourself lost or injured, there's no telling whether we'll be able to help you. Your fancy bloodline won't buy you any favors out here."

"Like it does anywhere," Nat muttered.

Sam couldn't offer anything to the question. Though her sister had married a nobleman, she had neither the bloodline nor the upbringing, much to Lily's dismay.

"I'll pretend I didn't hear you speak such, Mister Bowden. Few of the sailors would appreciate the culture talk you suffer through, but there's many who would want the navigation training, and few would turn down the fancy vittles, especially when supplies get low. You play chess with the captain while they labor. Don't think they don't notice. Whether they'd want to switch places or not matters little when you rest as they work."

Nat stared at the boards then, but unlike her, he didn't linger there. Instead, he stood up straighter than before. "I apologize for my ill-considered words, Mister Trupt. I'll work on schooling my tongue in the future."

The first mate gave him a slight smile, perhaps noticing how he'd kept from using an oath to give his words more weight. Sam only hoped Nat had not lost them the permission to go to the island she so wanted to explore.

Mister Trupt looked from one to the other of them. "Well? What are you waiting for? Gather your things and help with unloading the boat. You'll head back right after we eat, assuming you can be made ready."

Sam didn't wait another moment. She broke into a run for the hatch leading to both her prison and the one place she could call home, already running her meager possessions through her head. The blanket as they were unlikely to be ferried back until another load was ready, another set of trousers from what Nat had given her, and maybe...

Her mind stalled at the thought of tucking a spare gear or two into her pocket. She had none. What she'd stolen from the engineer she'd returned to protect Nat's neck. Any others she'd laid claim to were in her hands for a short while before she had to return the object they'd given her to fix.

"I'll see if there's a spare knife for you to use," Nat said, having come after her unnoticed. "If not, you can have mine." He swallowed hard, the first mate's warning clearly having sunk in.

Sam didn't want to explain what truly made her sigh, but she wouldn't take his knife without cause either. "I can fashion something out of wood."

He looked at her strangely. "The wood comes alive in your hands as well?"

Though not asked in fear, his question would surely provoke it if overheard. Luckily, Sam had no hesitation as she said, "Wood has a different kind of life in it. I work with aether when my bouts start. I didn't mean to do anything beyond stripping the bark as I've done a time or two to make a pry bar or the like. Nothing but metal draws the aether I need to make a change."

The relief on his face left her to wonder if he'd feared after all, but Nat said only, "I don't know what the sailors would do if they believed the actual boards at risk."

Then he took the bundle from her arms and twisted the blanket so it formed a sack of sorts. "Come on. I still have my things to gather."

11

N at tried to present a cool exterior as he and Samantha swung down the rope ladder into the shore boat. His efforts were helped by the distraction of her amazement.

From the way she tested her footing on the rope to how she gauged the stronger sway of the small boat, she acted as if she'd never been on a boat before. He knew she'd had a sheltered upbringing—as a Natural, she'd have had to—but to have never been on a vessel smaller than their ship seemed inconceivable.

"Oh, look, Nat. Those trees are so different from the ones at home. They have flowers growing from the bark itself."

He leaned over to get a closer look, and Sven had to catch his shirt so Nat didn't tumble over the side. All sorts of brightly colored fish swam through water so clear it rivaled the air. He gasped as much at the sight as almost swimming among them.

The big sailor gave Nat a wink and kept quiet, but Nat knew he'd failed to pretend any more sophistication than she had showed.

Sand grated against the bottom of the boat, and Nat was the first to spring over the edge into the shallow water. They had to tug the boat far enough up the beach so it wouldn't float away.

The boat held additional supplies for the shore team that had to be unloaded. The first few moments on this foreign soil were taken up with unpacking the boat and trucking the supplies to a rough hut designated for storage. The captain had clearly shared the word about Samantha's new look, because the sailors working alongside them made no comment. Nat caught them sending sideways glances in her direction still.

"A place as lush as this has its fill of pests," Seamus told them as he slapped a bug that came to rest on his neck. "Nothing's safe from them. The one good part of all these trees is their sap. It makes for strong caulking."

He jerked open the door to the storage hut and pointed out how they'd filled in the cracks between rough split boards with tree sap. "Doesn't keep out everything," Seamus told them as he closed the door, "what with people coming and going, but we lost a lot yesterday before we came up with this plan."

Nat took the time to admire the work they'd done, as Seamus clearly wanted, but he found Samantha's hand shadows using the light filtered through the translucent sap more amusing, especially when a rabbit peered over Seamus's shoulder at Nat.

He struggled not to laugh and offend the sailor, blurting out, "Is there much hunting? Rabbits, maybe?" to free his breath.

Seamus twisted a glance over his side, showing Nat hadn't been as successful in masking his amusement as he'd hoped, but he saw nothing with Samantha on the other side of the room. "Nothing like rabbits, or rats even, but we've caught a snake this wide round." He made a circle with both hands, showing a width bigger even than his thick neck.

"In the trees?" she asked, coming over to join them. Her eyes had widened in amazement, giving her an odd appearance with her pupils swelled in the dim light.

Seamus patted her on the head much like a small child or pet. "You better keep an eye out. They come right down from the trees, or up out of the water. Ground's none too steady in places either."

Nat shook his head. "Some paradise."

"It is what you make of it. Food, water, and wood to repair the ship. That's at least enough to take us safely into port. No better paradise to my mind."

Once they'd finished the unloading and stored their own supplies—limited as they might be—in one of the huts used for bunking down, Seamus took them on a tour of the site. He pointed out the latrine and where the crew scrubbed up in fresh water, a luxury none of them had seen for many weeks. Finally, he showed them where the galley stood, another caulked building, or rather two.

"There's seating enough inside the second one. It gets hot and close with a crowd of us sitting down for a meal, but better that than every other bite containing some insect or other. Already, one of the riggers lies sick. We don't know if he ate something bad or swallowed an insect but we couldn't find a mark on him. And so we eat inside. Can't stop the bites, but we can have our meals in peace."

As though to punctuate his statement, the sound of heavy retching overcame even the rush of waves up the beach.

Seamus nodded toward another building. "The surgeon works over there. You'd best do what you can to stay outside those walls. Captain will be taking on some new faces if this place has its way."

Nat caught a look of terror on Samantha's features only to see it drain away just as quickly as it had come. He wanted to curse the fate that made struggling to survive in a strange port better than adding new crew members who would be sure to discover the truth about her. More than just the crew's fickle nature made safety among strangers appealing, he supposed, and nothing he could do would make any difference.

"And that's the whole of it," Seamus concluded, unaware of the impact his previous statement had made on both of them. "Captain didn't assign you any tasks as of yet. Said you should have the chance to stretch your legs and shake off the sea first. Take care not to wander far, and keep your knife handy."

12

Seamus's warnings had clearly affected Nat, who wanted to stay so close they didn't cross the small river the sailor pointed out as a place to bathe. Even there he warned against submersion because of the man-sized water snakes and other reptiles nothing like the lizards at home.

Sam longed to go further and see more. She'd experienced little in her life so far, and hiding her nature in a foreign port would leave no time for exploring. Besides, she took Seamus's other words to heart. Paradise this was. Not because it held no dangers, but because it offered what she needed to distract herself from the uncertain future that loomed so close.

"We could follow one of the paths they've cut in the jungle," she said, pointing to the nearest rough-hewn opening in what seemed an almost solid wall of vegetation. "It wouldn't take us too far from the camp, and we could hardly get lost along it."

Nat gave the path a dubious look, glancing up at the branches overhead as well as forward to where even the sunlight took on a green tinge.

"Maybe we could find some of those flowers growing on the tree trunks. Cook sometimes used flowers to add a nip to her meals."

She smothered a laugh as Nat perked up a bit at the thought, his stomach no more impervious to the lure of tasty fare than any of the sailors. After several weeks living on the small amount he could secret away from his meals and drinking condensed steam from the engine, she'd found Jenson's cooking delectable, but starvation seemed the best spice of all.

"Just a little ways in. And on the path. Then we wait for one of the other sailors to be willing to come with us."

Sam nodded her agreement, already two steps closer to the opening she'd found. Between Seamus and Mister Trupt's warnings, she had no plans to wander further than she could find her way back, but having come so far, she couldn't spend her time sitting on the beach or huddled in the galley to get away from the persistent bugs.

She slapped one from her neck, sensing more than seeing Nat jerk at the sound. This had been the salvation he'd offered, for her, but for him as well. Somehow she didn't think he considered Robinson Crusoe realistic now, no more than he'd claimed the books with pirates to be.

"You think I'm a fool," he said, coming up next to her.

Heat rose to color her cheeks where she'd thought she'd masked her amusement. "No. Not really. I heard the same warnings, and it's not as if this place is a pleasure garden like Mister Trupt said."

He laughed. "But it's not a wolf-filled forest either. Still, I don't think we should go too far."

Relieved she hadn't alienated her one true friend, Sam grinned at him. "We won't. I promise. Just enough to get a feel for the place, so I know how it's not like those gardens."

"You've never been to a pleasure garden, have you?"

She didn't know how she'd given herself away, but then Nat had proven to be a careful listener. "I've read about them…"

"In Henry's library. He must be quite a wealthy man to have such an exhaustive collection."

Sam pretended not to have heard his teasing by speeding her step, then a glance ahead gave her a better reason to go faster.

"Wait up, Samantha. Not so far."

She turned back to call, "It's Sam," and when she faced front, her feet tangled beneath her. She went crashing to the ground, a pungent moss smeared on her hands and cheek.

"Samantha! Sam. Are you all right?"

Nat reached her side moments after she'd fallen. He grabbed first one leg then the other, feeling for broken bones or swelling she supposed. The touch made her face burn, but he seemed oblivious.

"I'm fine. I truly am. I just didn't look where I was going," she said as she pulled free of him.

Nat glanced up at her face, coming aware of his actions or so it seemed from how his own features reddened. "Are you sure?" His voice came out much softer and more hesitant.

Sam gave a firm nod. "I'm sure of it, I swear."

She paused, and they exchanged a laughing glance before she pushed to her feet.

"I really do swear. See, not even a limp." Sam took a few ginger steps, happy to find her assessment correct when she felt nothing but the twinge of quick-forming bruises.

"My fall really doesn't matter. Look there. Can you see it? One of the flowers. It's not far off the path."

Nat gave her one more looking over before he turned to follow her pointed finger. At first she thought he couldn't see the flash of color, but then his eyes narrowed and he stepped toward the tree with none of the nervousness of before.

"It looks close enough to the ground, though I may need to boost you if you're game."

"And what if I boost you?" Sam asked, hands on her hips.

He grinned. "Now that I'd like to see someday. Not here though. You might be strong enough to lift me, but I'm bigger, and I doubt you could carry me back to camp should I fall."

"What? You'd just toss me over your shoulder, I suppose?"

Nat reached for her, but she ducked out of his way.

"Like a sack of potatoes, I would."

Laughing, she twisted around him and stepped off the cleared path, determined to see this flower.

The jungle closed around them on all sides, hot, wet, and oh so close.

Sam's laughter choked off in her throat, and Nat said nothing more.

Strange cackles, clicks, and hums filled the air, while the shush of leaves rubbing together from the wind or the passage of a strange jungle beast reached her ears.

Suddenly, the warnings they'd received seemed ever more urgent.

Nat's hand closed around hers.

She half expected him to pull her back onto the path and wasn't completely sure she'd object if he did, but instead he leaned in close to whisper, "It's just a short way. Let's get the flower and go back."

Sam squared her shoulders and glanced up at the branches. How she'd make out a snake from a vine in the odd light, she had no idea. If only live wood gathered aether like metal. Then the dangers and treasures in this place would be lit from within, drawing her on. Instead, she had to depend on poor eyesight and memory.

"It's over there."

She hadn't expected Nat's skills as a spotter to work in the jungle for all that he'd told her how the riggers had been known to call him "sharp eyes" on occasion.

Any hesitation he'd had before vanished as he pulled her forward using their joined hands. Where leaves and speckled lighting confused her, he'd locked onto the flower much the way a hawk sights a rabbit, diving through the greenery as though unaware of anything but the target.

Sam tried her best to keep an eye out for snakes, but they were moving too quickly to see much of anything.

"There."

All of a sudden, he stopped. She slammed into his back before she could slow. He didn't seem to notice as he knelt at the base of a twisted tree trunk winding far up toward an unseen sky.

"Are you going to climb it or not?"

Sam hadn't realized she'd been staring dumbfounded until he spoke, but then she caught sight of the flower, so close and yet out of their reach.

She stepped onto his linked fingers and walked up the trunk with her hands as he rose.

It still teased from so short a distance.

"You're going to have to climb me."

With his hands to guide her, Sam planted first one foot then the other on his shoulders, a giggle escaping at the thought of how this would not have been possible, or at least not remotely proper, had she still been in skirts.

She tapped the bark hard twice, hoping to scare off anything that might be in the flower because she couldn't see so far above her head. Then, Sam reached up and plucked the blossom from the trunk with the force necessary to clip the stem.

Only instead of requiring a tug, it came as easily as if the flower rested against the tree rather than being a part of it.

She struggled to keep her balance, and Nat stepped back and to the side in an attempt to help her. Without the trunk's support, her precarious position became unstable.

"Easy now," he called up too late as one foot slipped from his shoulder.

Sam fell to sit with her legs straddling his neck, and his hands clasp hard on her thighs.

He knelt again, letting her slide free, then released a sigh of relief. "I thought for sure you'd topple off and hit your head."

Sam ignored his comment and held up the flower, which seemed more a distinct plant than a tree flower now that she got a better look at it. No wonder it had pulled free so easily.

"Now that's a beauty," Nat said, his voice low and reverent.

As though in agreement, a shrill voice called out from up in the trees, startling both of them.

Nat laughed first, but shook his head. "We better be getting back. We'll hear no end of it if the others have to waste time looking for us."

Sam tipped her head to one side. "If they even look."

Her position brought their path into view, and any fear of finding a way through to the cut swath vanished. They'd left a trail a blind man could follow, but they were neither blind nor so foolhardy as to remain in the jungle any longer.

The return trip had none of the tentative nature of their forward progress. Whether the flower offered a spice for Jenson or merely an interesting specimen to share with the captain, they didn't want to waste another moment before revealing what they'd found.

13

N at hadn't realized how long they'd been gone until they stepped free of the path to find the camp swarming with sailors who had been off on various tasks. They crossed to the galley hut to a chorus of teasing comments about Samantha's clothes and hair, but she only smiled in response.

Everyone seemed in a grand mood, so much so he wondered if the fruit they gnawed on had fermented.

"There you are," Seamus called from a nearby hut. "I'd started to wonder if the jungle beasts had swallowed you whole."

"Beasts?" Nat hated how his voice cracked on the word.

Phil came up from the side to swat Nat on the shoulder and peer at Samantha's cupped hands. "He's teasing, though the snake we caught was something else. What's that you have?"

The last he directed at Samantha, who opened her hands to show the blossom, though it seemed more a collection of stiff, colored leaves than a flower when Nat had looked at it up close.

"We're bringing it to Jenson," she told the rigger. "To see if he can use it in his cooking."

Phil barked a laugh. "Word spreads fast in a tight crew, Miss Samantha. There's none of us won't be happy to see you enter the galley…none but Jenson. I wouldn't expect much from him. If the captain couldn't get him to spice the food, he's not going to listen to a little slip like you."

She pressed her lips together in an expression Nat had come to learn didn't bode well for whatever stood in her path. Her pace quickened, and Phil didn't bother to stay alongside them.

Nat caught her arm and pulled Samantha to slow her down. "Remember what I said about the cook on a ship? Third in the crew's respect. If you want to aid him, best tread softly. And you sure don't want to cross him, especially not here when he could put who knows what in your bowl."

"He wouldn't!" Though her voice stayed firm, her eyes widened and a look of fear swept her face.

Nat shrugged. "I wouldn't want to test him."

Her forward progress stopped altogether with that. "What then are we to do with the flower? Why bother climbing up to fetch it if you weren't going to let me give it to him?"

"You could show it to him. Just don't expect much. And after he's scorned the offering, I'd guess you'd find a better audience with the captain."

She glanced at the galley and back to Nat. "We don't even know if it's any good in a meal. Just because some English flowers can work so doesn't mean this one can. Maybe we should go straight to the captain."

Nat hid his relief at this suggestion. He hadn't wanted to be on Jenson's bad side a second time on this voyage, and he suspected should Samantha put a foot wrong, the blame would fall firmly on his shoulders.

Besides, from the cheers and laughter over where the sailors had gathered, something worth investigating was taking place. The captain would be sure to be there while avoiding the galley might mean they avoided being roped into working in a hot, muggy hut as well.

A heavy thwack sounded and another cheer broke out.

Nat had never heard such merriment in the labor of chopping wood, and neither, apparently, had Samantha who made no objection to their change of path.

Sure enough, when they broke past the cluster of huts into a small clearing, Captain Paderwatch stood with the rest of the sailors as three worked their axes through some trees they'd felled.

The piece being split dropped open as they approached. Nat stopped dead to see such a rich purple tone to the wood.

The sailors cheered this split as well with a roar of sound.

Samantha crashed into Nat's back, having been looking ahead at the revealed wood rather than where she was going. They fell into a tangle of arms and legs, Samantha hindered by her efforts to keep the odd flower out of harm's way.

The sailors' cheering turned to laughter, and Nat reddened, knowing they found amusement at his expense. Before he could rise, though, the captain strode over.

The expected chastisement never happened. Instead, Captain Paderwatch paused to stare at the flower Samantha held lifted as if for his pleasure.

"What have you here?"

"It's a tree flower," Samantha and Nat said with one voice.

"We plucked it from one of the jungle trees," Nat added.

"Not plucked exactly." When the captain took the flower, Samantha twisted round until she could reach her feet. "It took hardly any effort at all."

The captain raised the flower up, examining it from all angles before he nodded. "That's a good observation. Look here.

Where you'd expect a broken stem, it has what could only be roots."

She leaned in close, extreme concentration on her face. "How can it have roots so high?"

The captain's eyebrows rose. "And how high was it?"

"Both my height and Nat's. He let me climb on his shoulders."

Captain Paderwatch's mouth twitched on one side. "He did, did he? Mister Bowden's usually the monkey from what I've seen on the ropes."

"I'm stronger," Nat muttered, not sure whether he spoke the truth for Samantha had shown no lack of resourcefulness.

"And I wanted to be the one to get it," she broke in to defend him. "I saw them as the boat brought us ashore and couldn't imagine why a tree would have flowers on its trunk instead of out on the branches."

The captain nodded. "You've solved the question now haven't you?"

Both Nat and Samantha looked at him then, and she tipped her head to one side.

"I have?" she asked.

Again he nodded. "This isn't a flower. Or at least not one belonging to that tree. As you said, it came too quick. Like moss or vines, I suspect it is a parasite. Or maybe a helpful companion."

Her expression didn't lighten with the explanation, but Nat had heard the captain speak of such before. "He means it feeds on the tree somehow, or maybe helps it."

Before she could ask any more questions, Phil, who had rejoined the others, called them over.

"Have you ever seen such color? It's in more of the trees than not."

Samantha knelt into the dirt, the better to poke at the revealed purple grain.

"Captain says it'll fetch something in trade, whether at the next port, or if we take it back to England. There's many a wealthy man might want some to line a parlor."

Nat could see his mother delighting in such a rich color without the need for paint or brocade.

"Don't touch."

He focused out of his thoughts to see Samantha frozen, her hand not a finger width from another log.

"She wouldn't harm it," he told Pennybright. "She can't work with wood. Tell them, Samantha."

"It's Sam," she said in a quiet voice. "But he's right. Growing things, even cut down, have a different kind of energy. Not like the aether metal works gather."

Pennybright shook his head. "I didn't think she would change it. That piece cut poorly and it oozes a sap not even ash can scrub from the fingers."

Sam pulled away from the log. She flashed the sailor a grateful smile, her look of fear gone.

Phil came up beside them to stare at the purple wood. "Sad thing is if she could shape this stuff, we'd be ten times as rich. Imagine coming into port with fancy goods all ready for some lady's home."

The others chorused in agreement, but she only shrugged.

"Shaped or not, you said the captain expects it to richen our shares," Nat said to distract them.

"That he did," someone called from the back. "We'll save any plain old brown wood we find for our repairs and collect a good measure of this purple to sell."

"Not too much," another added. "We have to be able to get to the port."

"Hush with such talk. Between our strong engine and the last of the spring storms most like behind us, not to mention the contraption the girl fixed to guide us through dark of night or storm either, we'll be at port before you know it."

"Not if we spend all our time chopping purple."

"We could come in with paddles bedecked like a fancy dock girl."

Nat and Sam wandered back over to the captain as the sailors continued with their calling, each trying to outdo the rest.

The captain glanced past them at the crew and laughed. "They're a rowdy bunch when they start counting coins that don't as yet exist."

Though Nat smiled, he had been making the same calculations in his head as well. The stronger his purse, the more he could push on Samantha when she had to go. Those coins from her sister's husband wouldn't last long, nor would they be enough to buy her a berth on a ship headed to England.

14

Talk over the meal was full of the trade goods they might discover. Beyond the purple wood, they had skinned the snake and were drying the iridescent leather.

The meat had gone into the evening's stew. Sam balked at this information at first, but when Nat dared her to try it, she found snake meat tasted like rather chewy chicken.

Everyone seemed to be enjoying their time on the island, especially Captain Paderwatch. Where the captain normally spent his time in the cabin from what she'd seen and heard, now he sat with the men, shared the same fare, and joined in with the discussion of not just what they could use the purple wood for but also what else they might find here.

"The flower you two pulled down could fetch a decent price, if we knew how to keep it alive," he told them. "You have only to look at orchids brought back from the new world to see the potential."

She promised to keep her eyes open to learn what she could about it, and Pennybright chopped a knot free of one of the felled logs to keep it in. A few splashes of water completed the effort, though Sam wondered if it needed the moisture at all when so much hung in the air.

When at last Sam entered the hut she shared with Nat and a handful of other sailors, she thought she'd have a hard time getting to sleep, but the excitement exhausted her. Before she knew it, morning had dawned.

Remembering Nat's caution, she stayed out of Jenson's way until breakfast was served, though if the cook noticed, he said nothing to her about it. Nor did he mention the cinnamon she'd taken from his stores.

Finally, they were ready to explore again.

The captain asked for two sailors to wander with them, and unexpectedly there'd been many volunteers. Or maybe not that unexpected.

Captain Paderwatch promised an extra share to the man who discovered something they could use to enrich their trade goods. Whether he planned on Nat having the flower share, should it survive, she didn't know.

The four of them, Phil and Hassan having drawn the choice to come, stood at the edge of the jungle and stared into its dark tangles.

"Come on then," Nat said. "Samantha—Sam—you choose the direction."

Hassan hefted a cutlass. "Whichever direction, I can cut us a path."

He seemed delighted at the prospect, but Sam hoped to explore further than they had the previous day. That meant using the efforts of the earlier adventurers once again.

She pointed to a path taking them in a new direction. "I'm sure we'll find use for your sword at some point."

He drew his mouth down in the mockery of a scowl. "The path leads to the purple wood. It's been tromped so many times anything interesting will be pounded into the soil."

Sam shrugged. "We'll just have to go past where they're chopping then."

Nat sent her a grin matching her own expression, and they left the sun-warmed clearing for the heavy, moist heat of the jungle.

Hassan got to use his cutlass faster than she would have thought possible. Vines already stretched across a space others must have slashed clear the day before, or within two days at the most. Nor did they see anything new.

They made so much noise blundering along, any interesting creatures would have had every opportunity to vanish into the thick growth, a fact Sam regretted at the same time she found it cheering.

A little adventure was all she sought. Snakes as big around as a man's upper arm could entertain the others while this little group went after exotic plants. Captain Paderwatch had warned against poisons, but at least plants would be unlikely to jump out of the shadows.

Sometimes she saw a flash of bright colors, and even caught a glimpse of the screeching birds once in a while, but for the most part, only plants offered themselves up for examination.

A strange rushing sound reached her ears, and Sam paused to glance around for a source.

The others stopped a few steps further on when they noticed, but soon they were all staring about.

Then a shower nearly as hot as came from Henry's pipes poured over Sam, dousing her hair and clothes within a heartbeat.

One of the sailors—she couldn't tell who—cursed the water, but she tipped her face up and embraced it. The sound had not meant snakes lurking in the shadows or even the big lizards some claimed to have seen. Instead, this water would wash away all the salt embedded in her skin during the ocean journey, and without risking dangers found in the water.

Having more in common with piped water than a rain shower, the water vanished as rapidly as it had appeared, leaving the lingering after-effects of its drenching in a series of pings and plops she now recognized as the rain falling on the treetops a mast's height or further above them before it trickled through the leaves on its way down.

Phil shook his whole body, tossing water left and right like a dog, but Hassan just stood there and grinned.

Nat, the source of the curse if his expression offered anything to go by, stripped his shirt to twist it dry.

Sam did not have the same luxury, but like Hassan, she found the drying water cooler than what filled the air around them.

"A jungle's abundant gifts," Hassan said. "Water all around, and yet it sees fit to offer us even more."

Sam shared a smile with him as they got moving again, this time her ears alert to any sounds that might give warning of another downpour. She didn't know if she'd step under shelter or further out to the center of the path should another shower of water arrive.

Nat felt the squish of mud beneath his feet with every step and despite wringing as much as he could from his shirt, the wet fabric showed no signs of drying. Even worse, the water in his trousers made the fabric chafe. Whatever craving he'd had to explore, right now he'd give anything for a patch of sunlight to dry his clothes.

As if to mock his wishes, he picked up a noise all too similar to the strange sounds they'd heard before the unplanned shower.

"And even more of her gifts," Hassan said, destroying any chance Nat had misheard.

"Don't be cursing the water, Mister Bowden," Phil added after a groan Nat hadn't realized he'd made. "Times enough when we'd have given anything for a rain shower."

"But not when the very air is dripping." Despite his words, Nat tipped his head up, determined to make the most of it.

Nothing came.

"It's not coming from up there." Sam's exclamation brought them all round to stare at her, at least until they figured out the same thing she had.

The drenching, it seemed, made them all a bit sensitive to the sound of water.

Hassan found a section just off the path where the jungle looked to be a tiny bit less dense. He raised the cutlass with a grin. "Stand back unless you fancy adding some red to this green."

She stuck her tongue out at him, showing how comfortable she'd grown. "I'd prefer to see colors on the backs of birds."

Phil came to stand between the two of them, well away from Hassan chopping. "Keep your eyes open for those birds. I doubt we'll be able to catch one, but if we can find any feathers, I'll bet they'd bring a pretty penny."

Her eyes widened as much as Nat's had. It seemed almost anything in this jungle offered a prize regardless of the discomfort required to claim it.

Nat tripped over his own thought, wondering how much this jungle would change once other trading vessels discovered it. The vines showed how quickly the island would wipe out all evidence of their presence, but could it do so if ten, or a hundred, times their number came to cull what they could of its treasures? He considered asking the captain to leave it off the charts returned to the company, though he knew Captain Paderwatch had already begun the records of this place and what could be found here.

"Are you coming?"

Sam's impatient voice jerked Nat back into the present where he discovered Hassan's entry point had been a guided choice. Through the gap he'd made, Nat could see a game trail not much different than the ones in England, or so he thought until Phil knelt to the ground and pointed at some markings in the soft soil.

"Look at these. Made by a giant lizard if I'd have to guess. See the deep claws, and how the marks are mostly obscured as if with a broom."

"Why would something that big have to hide its tracks?" Nat asked, leaning in to see better.

Phil gave him a look more like a slap on the head than anything else. "The marks come from a big, broad tail. Low to the ground, swishing back and forth."

Nat felt the heat of a flush rising as he recognized the truth in the answer, one he should have seen himself.

Sam sent him a sympathetic look and did the only thing she could to rescue him. She moved past all of them to follow the trail in the direction of the sound, leaving them to scramble after her.

They hadn't gone much further, though, than the source of the water noises became as obvious as the markings.

"A river," Hassan declared, stating what they all must have been thinking.

"I wonder if it's the same or a different one?"

Sam's comment barely crossed his ears as Nat pushed forward, seeing in the gap an answer to his prayers.

Phil caught his shoulder and held him back. "Remember the signs. I think we're not the only ones to seek this water."

Nat swallowed hard on the realization he could have ran straight into the jaws of a giant reptile.

"Lizards are slow in the sunlight," Sam said as she moved forward. "Maybe these are too. We just have to be careful."

Nat looked from one sailor to the other, and neither showed any sign of wanting to turn back. Perhaps he was not alone in the craving for sunlight.

All four of them, two abreast because of the width of the trail, set out again, and whether the giant lizard had come this way recently or not, they saw no sign of it.

"Stay clear of the water," Hassan warned.

Crossing to a pile of boulders off to one side, Nat said, "I have no intention of getting any wetter. I just want a moment to dry out."

Phil laughed, but Nat noticed he did not disagree.

The others joined Nat, and after a careful look around, they climbed on the rocks to bask much like the lizard they'd followed to get here would have.

Though he'd have given anything to get away from the heat before, something about direct sunlight offered comfort even as it converted the moisture on his clothing into steam. His mind wandered, and his eyes fogged over, a yawn surprising him. Nat didn't feel sleepy, exactly. More like embracing the slow, relaxing moment.

He glanced around to share the thought with the others, and jerked upright.

"Where's Samantha?"

16

Sam hadn't consciously decided to wander, but before she knew it, she'd slipped off the rock where she'd been sitting next to Nat and strolled down the river. At the edge of her attention, she'd heard whispers. Not quite voices, but something calling out to come and discover the source.

When she'd glanced back, it was to see the two sailors and Nat lying stretched out on the rocks. They seemed no more alive than the formations beneath them unless Sam watched long enough to note the movement of their chests as they breathed. It had been a long hike through the jungle even without the drenching. She didn't want to disturb them, especially since she was still in visual range.

The decision made, Sam gave the almost inaudible sound her full attention, both seeking it out and trying to follow it by instinct. Neither method offered enough confidence, but she didn't want to give up. What if she found some people living here deep in the jungle? Or maybe she'd found a new bird.

Those thoughts captured what little of her focus she hadn't devoted to the sound—or was it a sensation?—that drew her on.

The river rushed by on one side while the jungle threw its shadow over the water and offered up unexplained rustles. Still she went, slowly, quietly, always forward.

Her gaze swept the ground, the growth, and the water for any sign of what drew her on, but she couldn't identify the source until she stood right above it, a discovery so shocking she fell to her knees, or maybe the same whisper made her kneel so she could be closer to it.

Her fingers spread out along the rock face, a sloped section with embedded fragments of what almost looked like colored glass.

She brushed against one and her whole body sang with it.

Aether.

Sam had never known rock to gather the energy, and this stone held none of the consciousness metal seemed to carry. None of its demands.

She pressed harder until she lay across the surface, her skin touching as many of the odd fragments as she could.

Their voices sang to her, not demanding change or asking a thing of her. No, they just shared the moment, their songs clean, pure notes of strength. They knew what they were and why they lay there. They shared their confidence with her, filling Sam even as they welcomed her as she'd never been welcomed before.

"Samantha. Sam! Where are you?"

A new voice broke into her peaceful moment, cutting through the quiet stones with its sharp dissonance.

Sam wanted to ignore it, to snuggle tighter against the sun-warmed rock and bask in the demand-free aether, but the call sounded closer and closer until she could hear the beat of thick callused soles against the dirt at the river's edge.

"Here," Phil shouted. "She went this way."

She sat up just in time as the three of them burst around a turn she didn't remember making to stumble to a halt and gape at her.

Nat moved first, dropping to her side to look her over. "We thought you'd been taken. That the giant lizard got you. You should know better than to wander off. You are okay, right? You're not hurt?"

Part of her wanted to laugh at his non-stop questions, and part of her just wanted them to go away and leave her be. Luckily, she gave voice to neither urge and had them both under control by the time Nat wound down enough to let her get in a word.

"I'm fine. I followed the talking stones."

The sentence left her lips before she could call it back, suddenly protective of them, a ridiculous instinct when the stone held no value she could see, too fragile for some purposes and the muddy colors not bright enough to inspire avarice.

Nat glanced down at the rock face they now shared. "I thought just metal called to you."

He'd not only heard her words, but he'd understood them.

Sam shrugged. "I've never heard stone before this, but these have too little a voice to ask anything of me. I shouldn't have come here."

She pushed to her feet and took four steps back the way they'd come in the hopes he'd follow.

Instead, Nat brushed at one of the fragments. "Phil? Isn't this flint?"

The other sailors came to peer down at the rock as well, their voices sharp with excitement.

Sam didn't bother to hear their words, especially when the scrape of a metal knife against stone sent a jarring stab through her ears and down her back. She wanted to cry out, to protest, but could only stand numb as one of the singing voices cut off, its peace and hers destroyed in a heartbeat.

"Careful. It'll send up sparks."

"As wet as the jungle is here, fire is the least of our worries."

"The captain will be pleased with this find, for sure."

Their voices filtered in through her numb shock as the aether-raised tones snapped one after the other like the strings of a violin played too often with vigor.

"That's the last of them," Hassan declared, stepping back to display what had been a smooth surface and now lay gutted, pitted, and torn apart.

Had it been an animal, the ground would have been deep red with blood. Instead, the only blood lay pounding against her ears where the song had been such a short time earlier.

"You found it, Samantha. You should have the first stone."

Something smooth pressed against her palm, but when her fingers closed around it, the sharp edge sliced her flesh, as sharp as the realization of what Nat had placed there.

She gave a wordless cry, threw the deadened stone as far from her as she could manage, and took off back the way they'd come with no thought beyond getting away from those who had taken her peace and shattered it, all in the name of a heavier purse.

17

I t took a moment before Nat processed what had happened. He glanced to Phil and Hassan, half sure he'd made the whole thing up, but once again, Sam was gone.

"We've got these. You go after her," Phil said.

As if released from paralysis, Nat moved then, but not in the direction she'd gone. Instead, driven by instinct, he searched the ground for the flint she'd thrown away. He shoved it into his pocket, waved at the other two, and sprinted back up the river.

He half expected to find her waiting for him at the rocks, but there was no sign she'd stopped. He wished he had Phil's tracking ability so he could have known for sure, but he had to keep going anyway. He wouldn't rest until he found her.

The way seemed much longer than when they'd gone to the river despite the effort required to cut through and not knowing where they were going. He reached the join to the main path after what seemed forever and still she wasn't there.

Finally, after Nat almost turned back to see if she'd gone a different way, he caught a glimpse of her burnt orange-flame hair further along the trail.

Nat pushed harder, his feet pounding against the still-damp earth. The distance between them began to narrow. It helped that she no longer ran wild but had slowed to a walk.

Still, when he reached her side, they were only a few yards from the camp.

He moved into step beside her and glanced toward Samantha, but she didn't look at him. She didn't react to his presence at all.

With the worry of something having befallen her gone, Nat struggled to figure out what had happened. She didn't seem hurt. She didn't have the look about her when she used her Natural abilities. She didn't seem different at all.

But still she wouldn't look at him.

Nat reached a hand over to stop her, but she flinched from his touch, moving closer to the jungle rather than staying at his side.

"I'm sorry," Nat said. "I don't know for what, but I'm sorry."

She shook her head in answer and sped up.

Nat caught her arm, this time before she could duck. "Tell me what's wrong."

She threw up both hands as if to ward him off, her eyes looking anywhere but at him.

This time he thought he detected something of the strange nature that took her over when using her knack, but it could have been wishful thinking.

He let go, exhausted all of a sudden, but when her hands dropped away, he snagged one to bring it closer. "You are hurt."

"It doesn't matter."

Her voice sounded flat and sad all at once.

Nat stared at her palm and the slice cut into her skin. "There's even greater chance of infection here. It's not worth risking the loss of a hand."

Her injury offered what he clearly could not, a way to help make up for whatever he'd done. Even when she tried to tug free, he kept the hold as he pulled her toward the galley.

After a bit, she stopped resisting, but he had to make do with that as his only concession.

"Jenson? Do you have any water gone hot?"

Nat called the question even as he shoved through the doorway, pulling her in after him.

A fire pit sat in the very center of the hut, smoke rising through a hole in the roof. Over the fire, Jenson had rigged a frame on which hung a kettle, steam just starting to spill from its spout. Of the cook, he saw no sign.

"Sit." He shoved her down at the sole table surrounded with rough-hewn benches.

She sat.

He could feel her numb stare on his back as he found a cup and poured some of the water. He'd sear her with a worse injury than the clean slice if he didn't let it cool a little.

Nat sat opposite Sam, the cup of hot water between them. He wanted to say something, to do something, to mend the breach between them, but her expression stayed closed, holding him silent.

Finally, he splashed some water on his wrist and found it hot but not too hot.

"Your hand." As with his earlier command, he made no attempt at conversation. She'd rejected the stone he'd given her, and he didn't want to risk rejection a second time.

When she didn't react, he put his hand on the table palm up and stared at her.

She still refused to meet his gaze, but her arm moved slowly, then she laid her hand in his, the touch so slight his eyes knew before he could feel her skin resting against his.

Nat didn't wait another moment before upending the cup over their combined hands.

He sucked in a sharp breath at the contact, the water hotter than he'd expected.

When she tried to pull free, he closed his fingers around her and watched the water pour from her skin. She had not been cut by a stray branch or when she'd fallen. The slice lay too clean and too precise.

His gut twisted with the realization he'd done this to her. She'd been cut with the flint he'd given her. Only flint had a fine enough edge, as sharp as any sailor's knife.

Now he knew what he'd done.

Before he could tell her, though, a shout cut the silence between them. A call for the surgeon. Both he and Sam leapt to their feet and were halfway to the door without exchanging a word.

No sailor would call for the surgeon unless at death's door.

18

Nat scrambled out of the galley and ran toward the sound, Sam right beside him, though he had no idea how they could help.

"Get the surgeon," came the shout one more time, but it didn't hold the panic he would have expected.

They followed the voice to the clearing's far end in time to join a crowd ready to welcome, or mourn, those coming out of the forest.

Seamus came through first, looking much like an ancient savage with a bloody pelt slung over his shoulders and a big grin on his face.

Nat glanced around at the others to see the same confusion. The sailor seemed more likely to seek congratulations than a surgeon's bloody knife.

"Well," he said, looking around at the crowd. "Where's the surgeon?"

The sullen old man pulled forward from the gathered sailors. Both age and general disposition made him unable to find a better post, though his skills didn't do him any favors. He had no friends among the crew as far as Nat could tell.

"Yr not looking any worse for wear, Seamus. What you causing all this ruckus for?"

"It's not for me." Seamus knelt to drop the skin to the ground. "I'm to get you ready while the others heft a stretcher through the jungle."

As if one being, they all swiveled to stare down the path, Seamus included.

"I didn't think they'd fallen so far behind," the big sailor muttered. "I'll head back and give them a hand."

Captain Paderwatch appeared out of nowhere, or so it seemed, to clasp Seamus on the arm. A heartbeat later, he withdrew the touch and wrinkled his nose in disgust. "You're not going anywhere. You need to wash the blood off that pelt, or burn it off, and from yourself as well. Whatever wore the coat before you must be the cause of the stretcher. We don't want to draw more of the same here."

Seamus had been looking surly up until the last. His gaze dropped to the ground, whether to gauge the extent of the blood droppings or in shame, Nat couldn't tell.

"You two. Help this man with his prize. Look sharp now. And you four go relieve those with the stretcher."

Nat would have been willing to undertake either charge, but the captain pointed to others in the crowd before taking his handkerchief and scrubbing it against the contaminated palm.

"I can help," Nat said, moving to the captain's side.

Captain Paderwatch gave him a long look, then just when Nat had given up hope, he nodded. "You can draw some more fresh water from the river and put it on to boil. I'd guess those coming in next will have worked up quite a thirst, and the surgeon will have need of the boiled."

While it wasn't what he might have hoped for, Nat didn't wait for further instructions. He heard the captain calling to others to dig up the contaminated dirt and bring it down to the ocean before he moved out of earshot to grab one of the buckets left by the galley the last time a water run had been performed.

The thunk of the second bucket caught his attention only to find Samantha at his side. Still silent, she took on the task as well.

He ducked his head to hide a relieved smile. They had more mending to do, or so he suspected, but at least he could see a reason to hope.

19

Sam followed Nat down to the river and knelt at his side, unable to free her tongue after how she'd behaved. At first, righteous anger kept her silent and fuming, but she'd already started to recognize how childish her behavior had been before he caught up with her. For him to tend her cut despite everything only made her actions less worthy.

She'd known exactly why they went into the jungle. Sure, exploring had been a part of it, but she'd been just as eager as the others to find something new, something exciting. Hadn't she been the one to tear down the flower with no thought to its survival? And what of the snake meat she'd filled her belly with. Her objections there had been to its strange nature not to the death that made her meal possible.

To lose her friend over a glimmer of aether was the height of stupidity.

Her one excuse, as flimsy as it might be, was that in lying against the stones she must have bonded with them much like her mechanical creatures felt tied to her. They'd do anything to be at her side, why she'd secured the door of the workshop Henry had made her with every little mechanical inside. She'd had to lock them up not just because their presence would have endangered Henry and Lily but because if they'd tried to follow her across the ocean, the salt would have corroded them.

Her reasons had been sound then, and nothing had changed, but she missed the feeling of her creatures around her. The ones she tended on the ship already had connections, like the way Henry's pocket watch had chosen him once she'd given it self-awareness rather than becoming hers. Either that, or somehow limiting herself to restoring the original purpose prevented any bond from forming.

She didn't know the answers. All she knew was those stones with their complacent aether had eased a pain she hadn't realized she been suffering, and when the tie had been cut, she'd felt the loss with every fragment of her being.

Water sloshed against her leg as she carried the heavy bucket back to the galley. Ahead of her, Nat showed the same difficulty in keeping his bucket steady. They'd need a few more trips before the kettle would be full at this rate, as large as it was, and first they had to tip out the water already steaming there.

It seemed cruel to keep Nat unaware of her change in mood, though worse if he thought his apology accepted.

He had done nothing wrong.

Nat held the door for her, and Sam sent him a slight smile as she passed.

They didn't have time to repair their friendship just yet, but once the water had been collected, she'd pull him aside. She'd ask him for the rock. Asking should be enough because she knew he'd come right after her. He wouldn't have it. She could tell him not to worry, and they would be back where they had been.

As plans went, it had little complexity, and yet still she was foiled by the many other tasks they were drawn into. Eventually, though, she found herself alone with Nat and no responsibilities waiting to pull them off again.

Nat rubbed a hand across his sweaty brow. "That's the last of it for a bit, I think." He sank down on a nearby rock, their tasks having ended with them both outside.

Sam remained standing, shifting her weight from one foot to the other. It had seemed so easy in her head, but what if he didn't want to hear her out? What if he'd taken all he could from her and this had been the last straw?

"Aren't you tired?"

She stared at the hand he tapped on the rock beside him. He wouldn't talk this way, act this way, if he didn't still like her. She just had to get this over with before she made things worse.

"Can I have the stone?" The words blurted from her lips with none of the care she'd intended, leaving her staring at him like a mad thing. She'd made a demand she knew he wouldn't be able to fill, and she didn't want him to, but he didn't know that.

Sam swallowed hard and tried again. "I mean, I'm sorry I threw away your gift. I'd be happy to have it."

Her stilted words might not have sounded any better, but at least now he knew which stone she'd meant, rather than thinking she wanted to oust him from the rock where he sat. Sam watched him, waiting for him to tell her it was lost in the jungle so she could dismiss the idea and be done with it.

Instead, he leapt up and dug into his trouser pocket. "I am surely glad to hear you say that, Samantha. I was worried I'd done something horrible."

She tried to catch his gaze so she could wave off the need, but he twisted to concentrate harder. Then he pulled forth the one thing she had been sure she'd never have to suffer again.

His lips shifted into a hope-filled smile as he proffered the stone.

Sam could not compound her error. She'd just have to find a good burial spot because she refused to lose Nat over this.

She gritted her teeth, pulled her lips into a grin of sorts, and raised her palm to accept the dead thing from him.

Whether she'd done a better job of acting than she thought, or he'd been too relieved to notice, Nat didn't seem to sense anything out of order as he dropped the stone onto her flesh.

A surge of aether brushed her, aether feeling like Nat himself. It carried his worry and care for her.

Sam jerked, tossing the stone to the ground at her feet.

Nat pulled back with a frown. "What is it about the stone?"

Rather than answer his question, Sam knelt into the dirt to capture the gift once again. She held it tight to her chest. The aether whispered to her, comforting her and bringing with it the essence that was Nat.

They had not killed the stone after all when pulling it from the bigger rock.

This precious stone would be there to comfort her after she'd left the ship to find her own way. It would keep Nat with her once he'd returned to the sea.

Nat stared at Samantha, his hurt forgotten as confusion took its place. Whatever drove her, the stone could not be the simple gift he'd thought it. First she cast it aside, and now she cradled the stone like a baby.

He bent to brush her shoulder, and she startled enough to fall back on her heels, her thoughts far from this place, and far from him.

"What is it about the stone?" he asked again once she focused on him. "Why do you keep throwing it away?"

Unlike her previous strained effort, this smile she gave him held nothing but delight. "It gathers aether. You tore it from the rock and the aether was gone."

He'd listened to her often enough to understand she saw the aether gathered by these things much like a soul. The truth of what he'd done sank in.

"I killed it."

She shook her head vigorously, still clutching the stone to her breast. "I thought so. I really did. But you didn't kill it. You held it. You gave it something of yourself."

Nat moved back a step, staring at her with an uncomfortable feeling in the pit of his stomach. "It took some of my soul?"

Her laugh cut through the air, shocking him. "Not your soul. Aether is everywhere around us. It's a part of existence. The stone gathers its own."

He looked at her, still not comforted. "You said it took something."

Sam held out a hand, and he pulled her upright, noticing she made no effort to release her grip on the stone. She moved to the rock he'd been using as a bench, and much like he had, patted it for him to join her.

Nat sank down, his head lowered into his hands. He felt no less whole, but he wondered if he had it in him to notice.

She brushed his shoulder until he twisted to face her.

"It didn't take something. You gave it something. You pushed your thoughts of me, your worries, out into the aether. The rock collected what aether you had filled with your concerns."

That didn't sound as bad as he'd thought, until he considered the whole of what she said. Heat rose up the back of his neck. "You can read my thoughts with the stone?" He half wanted to snatch it away.

As if aware of his inclination, she tightened her grip then gave a soft cry.

He grabbed her hand and peeled back each finger. This time the edge had only pinkened her flesh, not cut through.

"I'm fine," she said, closing her fingers around the stone again, "And I can't read your thoughts. I can't even read what you thought when you had the stone. It's not like that."

Relieved, he gave her a lopsided smile as an apology for his suspicions. "Then what is it like?"

She shrugged. "I don't know if I can explain it. I can feel the sense of you. Not words or anything, just…well…it feels like you do. And it cares about me."

He coughed at the last bit, but she could hardly doubt his care. "Well, that's all right then, I guess."

Sam gave him a wide grin. "It's better than all right. It means when I leave at the port, I'll still have something of you with me. I won't be alone."

Nat put his head back into his hands to hide his expression. He should be happy for her, but every time he thought about her going into a strange port without anyone to watch out for her, his chest burned. If he could only come up with a better plan, he would, but nothing came to mind beyond the crazy thought of running away here on the island and making their home together in isolation.

The surgeon took that moment to step outside his hut and announce, "Pennybright's sewn up as best as I can make him. If he survives the night, he should make it to the next port."

The open door released a stench of blood and burnt flesh strong enough to choke them where they sat.

Nat rose, pulling her with him. "Let's go help Jenson get the meal on."

It had been the first thing to pop into his head, but the way his stomach turned over with the thought made him regret it. Still, better that than suffer the grisly discussion sure to follow the surgeon's comment.

When they neared the galley, they found Jenson already had as much help as he could use, and many others besides.

"He had deep claw marks down one side. Almost tore his leg off right there," Seamus said, waving a clawed hand still attached to the newly cleaned pelt. "Might not look like it now, but this jungle cat sure was fast and smart too. Wouldn't have caught it but for how it snagged a claw in Pennybright's belt."

"Uh huh," added one of the other sailors. "This here jungle has a mess of dangers mixed in with its beauty. Paradise sure, but not a welcoming one. We needs to be back on the ship and on our way if you get my meaning."

Jenson nodded a greeting to Nat and Sam. "You come to help? This lot's more interested in talking up our ends than filling our bellies."

Caught, Nat couldn't very well say no, especially not with how Sam moved forward to join the cook, eager, he guessed, to make it clear she did not consider herself his better because of the cinnamon.

Swinging the hut door open, Jenson waved them through then shut the door firmly behind them.

"They're right, you know," the cook said as he pulled out some odd-looking roots for them to peel. "We shouldn't linger. There's too much we don't know about this place. Too many dangers. We've been lucky, though I doubt Pennybright's going to think so when he wakes up without a leg. And there's others who are still shaking from the insect-bite fevers."

"At least there's a lot of worthwhile trade goods to be found here," Nat said. He paused, wondering how Sam felt about the other stones. Would they hold a bit of Phil and Hassan within them like hers held him?

Jenson shrugged even as he pulled forth more of the snake meat. "Sure, we've added to the cargo a good bit of value. No one's disputing that. But there comes a time to accept we've taken what we need and not keep going back for more. A man's greed is his downfall. I have no intention of letting some jungle cat take a chunk out of me just for a few extra coins. No sir. I have enough squirreled away already and it's only good if I'm alive to see to the spending of it."

21

It seemed the captain shared Jenson's opinion.

Sam listened to plans to pack everything up and return to the ship the next morning, dusk having already fallen by the time everyone sat down to eat. They would complete what they could of the repairs already begun on the ship, those possible without a dock, and head to the nearest port for the rest.

She slipped her hand into the pocket where Nat's stone rested, drawing strength from his imprint as she would have to soon enough.

The dangers of this place had come to outweigh the potential discoveries. She couldn't disagree with the assessment, but at the same time, the dangers that faced her once they landed at a port held as much fear as any she could find for the wild creatures in this jungle.

Her bread lay soaking in the stew, reminding her of how she wouldn't have survived as a stowaway without Nat cutting his own rations to feed her. She'd truly be on her own once Nat sailed off to the next port.

Sam lifted the bread to her lips, having learned the hard way not to waste food. She missed the days of sitting in Cook's kitchen, gobbling down whatever the kindly woman decided to make just to see the sparkle in Sam's eyes.

A deep homesickness struck her then.

She'd sometimes thought of her limited life like a prison of sorts when she couldn't leave the estate. More than one of Henry's staff looked at her with fear in their eyes as well.

How little she'd understood her freedom. Limited it was, but she had as many friends among those who worked on the estate as feared her, and she had a family to comfort and protect her.

Here, she had only Nat, yet he had become something unknown to her before. Both a friend and an equal.

She'd done more to endanger him than keep him safe, but he still stood at her side and listened while she tried to explain what made her the way she was.

No one, not even her sister Lily, had ever asked about what it meant to be a Natural. Her talent had been the family secret. All those on the estate had known about her, but they never spoke of it if they could avoid saying anything. They pretended her Natural abilities didn't exist.

Nat, though, he wondered. And he'd never been one to keep his counsel when he could discover something new. They shared a kinship in curiosity where they had no other tie.

The stew tasted sour against her tongue, no fault of Jenson's but more because she knew just what fate offered her now.

Sam stood, bowl in hand, and wandered out of the meal hut to stare into the jungle.

She'd rejected Nat's crazy idea before, but would it be so much worse here? She couldn't ask him to join her. She'd be truly on her own.

But from how the crew spoke of the purple wood and other discoveries, even the stones, they'd be sure to return. At least she'd have something to look forward to, and no one would be trying to capture her and lock her up. She wouldn't have to hide her nature here where she had none to hide it from.

Her fingers stroked the stone again. The collected aether promised her company of a sort. If she could find stone like this, perhaps she'd find a grain of metal close enough to the surface. She'd never created something from nothing before. She could surround herself with mechanicals, let them roam free in the jungle, and no one would call her out for it.

Without thinking, she took a step toward the dark trees.

A hand closed on her arm, holding her back. "You weren't sneaking off, were you?"

Nat clearly tried to sound like he was joking, but the tension in his fingers called out the lie. "At least wait until morning when you can see the jungle cats."

Sam glanced at the dark jungle once more then turned to face her friend. "It would solve all our problems."

Nat shook his head so hard his curls bounced. "It would not solve the least of our problems, especially if you went off on your own. Do you know how much trouble I'd be in when I called a halt to the plans to leave so we could find you and drag you back? Or how much trouble Captain Paderwatch would be in with my mother if I decided to find you myself?"

Her gaze dropped to the dirt, though barely enough light remained for Sam to see her feet. She needed no reminder of the disasters that followed wherever she went.

"I could live in the huts. I wouldn't cause any more trouble on the ship, and I wouldn't get in trouble at the port either. I'd be safe here."

Nat gave a sour laugh, grabbing her chin to pull it up so she had to face him. "You forget the captain has us leaving because too many of the crew are sick with fevers from the bug bites. And Pennybright will be lucky to survive his injuries. It'll be a long time before he's ready to crew another ship. No one is safe here."

She planted a fist on each hip. "It was your idea to start out with."

"A crazy idea. You dismissed it then before even seeing the island. Now, it's more obviously a flawed plan than before, and you think to take it on?"

"How would you stop me?"

He scowled back at her. "I'd tell the captain. He won't have you on his conscience any more than you already are. He'll bundle you up and row you out to the ship himself if that's what it takes."

Sam glared at Nat for a moment longer before an image of the captain rowing a shore boat on his own reached her mind.

A chuckle broke free, followed by another, and soon Nat joined in.

"I wasn't really thinking it," she said after a bit. "I mean, I was, but not so as to actually do it. There's much to value in staying here, but I'm not as good a cook as Jenson. Like as not, I'd swell my stomach on too many sweet fruits and explode."

He linked an arm with hers and tugged her toward the kitchen where Jenson had wash water waiting for the dish she still carried. "As much as some would pay to see the show, it's better you stay with others of your kind."

Her humor dropped away, and she pulled free. "There are no others of my kind, not that I know of at least."

Nat let her go, but not too far. "Your kind is human as well you know. Your gift makes you different, but it doesn't change what you are. This place is meant for wildlife. Even in the worst of your bouts, you're not wild."

Sam had to take what comfort she could from his statement. Nat knew what she was and what she could do better than any beyond her family, and in some ways better even than they did. If he could see her as a person, then perhaps she could act enough like one to survive.

She had some measure of skill beyond her Natural instincts but only if she could keep herself under enough control to use it.

22

*M*orning dawned into controlled chaos as the sailors stripped the little camp of everything portable, leaving only the huts to show they'd been there at all. With Mister Trupt supervising the repairs on the ship, the captain and Jenson shared command of the process.

Sam ran after Nat, helping where she could and otherwise trying to stay out of the way. Had she still wanted to vanish, as busy as everyone was, she could have done so easily. Nothing had changed since the night before. Neither her reasons to stay nor the very real reasons not to. She had but to recognize how much she enjoyed the bustle of the sailors with their rough words and ready smiles to know she'd never be happy here all by herself.

The irony was not lost on her.

She had left one location because it held too little joy, though the choice had not been hers to make, and now she left another for the same reason. But the third time would not hold mixed feelings. Despite Mister Garth's animosity and fearing the crew would turn on her, she'd been happy on Captain Paderwatch's ship, as happy as ever before.

"Come on, Samantha. It's our turn to ferry back to the ship."

She stared at Nat blankly, too caught up in her thoughts to understand him until too late to correct his slip on her name.

He grabbed her arm. "You're not still thinking of staying here, are you? It's not safe. I won't come back this way to find your gnawed bones tossed around like so many sticks."

Sam shuddered at the image, but she couldn't let it pass so easily. "Better you come back to the port and visit me in an asylum? Death might be kinder."

Nat grabbed her other arm until he held her caged. "Never say that. Never. Not even as a joke. From death there's no escape. No hope. I have faith in you. You'll be able to manage the port. You've done so well on the ship once you were out of the engine room. You need only avoid mechanicals and you'll be just like any other girl."

A laugh bubbled up where she'd thought no humor remained.

"Don't you mean like any other boy?" she said, tugging on the short queue she now wore in place of her long hair.

His expression didn't soften as he stared down at her.

Sam shook her head. "I didn't mean it. Any of it. I have no more intention of staying on this island forever than the captain has of signing me on as a permanent member of the crew."

She glanced over his shoulder to the waiting shore boat. "Shouldn't we go take our places? We wouldn't want the captain waiting on us."

Nat's shoulders relaxed as he let her go to snatch up his bundle and toss hers to Sam. "No, we wouldn't want them waiting. They might decide to leave us to the jungle cats and snakes after all."

Sam shot him a smile, grateful as always for his quick forgiveness. She'd miss many of those who lived aboard this ship, but Nat most of all.

Her free hand reached to brush the stone as she stepped into the shore boat, almost causing her to stumble.

Seamus, already seated on the bench, caught her arm and tugged her the rest of the way with ease.

"Thank you," she murmured, moving forward so Nat could follow. If only the sailors would accept her as easily as they seemed to. The thought blew away like a morning fog, too impossible to linger.

23

From the moment he climbed out of the shore boat and up the rope ladder to the deck, Nat could tell something was up. More than one of the sailors bore the expression of one dying from the agony of keeping a secret.

He watched carefully as he and Sam helped unload their boat, wondering where he'd find a snake, or lizard, or a pile of the seeds that emitted a stench worse than a dead cow left to rot for days in the field if disturbed, or so Seamus claimed.

When he'd joined the crew, there had been pranks a plenty. He'd thought them inspired by envy at first, but soon learned none among the crew envied him his fancy clothes or clean diction. Not a one of them wouldn't have wanted a heavier purse, sure, but to give up the sailing life and live within the strictures high society maintained despite the changes never crossed their minds. Nat understood how they felt now, the motion of the sea as much a part of him as breathing.

"Look lively, Mister Bowden. Shore leave has ended and there's work to do," Sam called, mimicking Mister Trupt.

A flush heated Nat's cheeks as he realized he'd been standing in the way, his mind focused on the past. "Yes, sir," he said, reaching for the next stack of rough planks.

Sam gave him a grin as she passed him, comfortable enough to join the crew in having its fun. He half wondered if she, not the hardened sailors, was behind whatever had them fit to burst.

As the day wore on, with task after task assigned him and Sam with him, he decided he'd been mistaken. If they'd decorated his hammock with one of the reptiles, he'd most likely fail to notice when he finally crashed down for his rest.

Jenson pulled the big stew pot out onto deck for their evening meal, the gleanings from the island now stowed and critical repairs complete. Nat was not the only one with slumped shoulders and dragging feet who lined up for the meal.

"I wonder if you're thinking you would've been better off back on the island," he murmured to Sam.

She shook her head, strands pulled loose from her queue swinging forward to frame her face and wipe out any attempt at boyish looks despite the smear of dirt across one cheekbone.

He stared at her, half forgetting the question until she spoke.

"This ship and its crew are worth the work I've done today and before now." A blush colored her face, and she stared at the deck, one toe twisting against the wood grain. "I've never had so many people be nice to me, welcoming even."

Nat stared all the harder, this time not cataloging her appearance but running the day through in his mind. She'd been with him like a shadow ever since they reached the ship. Where he'd been seeing a prank waiting to be discovered, could they have been smiling at Sam? Being welcoming as she said?

The whole of the day rewrote itself along very different lines.

He couldn't remember a single sour look sent in her direction. No one pulled away or avoided her as she carried out the tasks of one of the crew. At the same time, they didn't treat her as something different either. Somehow, when he hadn't been paying attention, she'd gone from superstition-based luck charm to a junior member, and he could credit the transformation to her willingness to lend a hand to whatever task they gave him.

The two of them shifted forward with the line, but now Nat focused less on his own weariness and more on the way the sailors aimed a nod or a smile in Nat's general direction when they passed. Or they called out some comment to Sam about the events of the day. It seemed the trip to her island, despite Pennybright's injuries and the fevers, had softened their mood and gave her standing where before she'd had none beyond a dangerous curiosity.

"It's not cinnamon porridge," Jenson said, doling out a serving to Sam, "But it's what you'll get."

She gave the cook a grin. "I'm starved for one of your hearty stews. Porridge would barely line my stomach."

Jenson paused at her response then poured another scoopful into her bowl. "Glad to hear it. Them sailors had me thinking you too delicate for a man's fare."

She laughed so hard the others turned to see what caused the ruckus. Jenson seemed to have forgotten, or chose to ignore, her female nature. If the cook could think her a boy with a man's appetite, maybe she would be able to make her way at the port after all.

They settled down to eat with the riggers, and Sam put action to words as she shoveled the stew into her mouth as fast as any of them.

Nat had to admit himself too hungry and too tired to taste much of anything. His bread scraped the bottom of his bowl well before he expected it, and a yawn stretched his mouth wide. He glanced over to see Sam in nearly the same state, or a worse one as her cleaned bowl slipped from a lax hand to bounce on the deck.

"Come on," he said. "Time to settle down for the night. I'll be up with first watch if you want to join me."

She stumbled to her feet, but even her struggle wasn't enough to mask how all those close enough to hear froze.

Suddenly Nat realized he'd been right in the expectation of a prank, only he wasn't the target.

He'd take Sam down to her room and deal with whatever they'd done. He hadn't understood when they practiced such trickery on him, but he'd make sure she knew it was a matter of affection. He wouldn't let her do anything to jeopardize the welcome she so appreciated.

From what she'd told him, her opportunities for such welcome had been few and far between, if she'd ever felt such from those without a blood tie.

*J*enson's rich stew settled into Sam's stomach and dragged her faster toward sleep than she'd ever been even after transforming a large mechanism in a full bout. Their labors throughout the day had been distinct enough she never stopped to notice how endless they'd become. Buoyed on the crew's apparent acceptance, she could have accomplished anything.

Now all the work weighed her down.

She couldn't stop yawning even after she stumbled behind Nat to return the bowl and thank the cook for a delicious meal. It seemed she'd managed to mend whatever harm the crew's appreciation of her porridge might have caused. Jenson went so far as to suggest she show him what she'd done.

"Tomorrow, if you don't mind," she replied, her words slurred by yet another yawn.

Jenson laughed at her then. "Tomorrow's soon enough. For now, you should seek your hammock before you take a tumble off the deck and we have to fish you out of the water."

Sam gave him a weak smile as she headed for the stairs down to the bilge room. Tonight even its unpleasant odors would make little impact. She'd sleep in two feet of water if given the chance to close her eyes.

Nat came with her, pausing long enough to light a lantern.

She didn't know whether choice or the captain's order drew him, so swallowed the suggestion he seek his own bed. When she squinted in his direction, he looked no less worn. If not for how hard every person on the crew had worked, she'd have suspected them of pushing more of the burden on Nat, and by inference on her, for them to be so exhausted.

Sam stopped at the door, stepping back for Nat to unlock it, something that would explain his presence better than either desire or command.

He twisted the handle without using the key. When he swung the door wide, Nat lifted the lantern up high as if looking for something hidden.

She peered over his shoulder only to gasp in surprise, her exhaustion melting away.

The place she'd half dreaded returning to after the island's clear air had been completely transformed.

Sam nudged Nat out of the way to investigate her new quarters. They'd undergone such a change, new seemed the best word to describe them despite existing in the same space. She stumbled on the first step, not because of any tiredness but because the floor now met the walls a good half-foot higher than before, above where the stains showed water had a tendency to collect.

The indrawn breath of her gasp had hinted at what she would discover next in the light shed by Nat's lantern. The crew had painted the very walls with a pungent sap from the island, not the one used to seal cracks in the huts but rather one whose scent resembled freshly crushed mint leaves.

She breathed deep to confirm no hint of the lingering stench remained.

Even the short table had been replaced with one of a decent height made from the purple wood. Her things had vanished into a small chest. Though simple, with fiber hinges and a latch made of knotted rope, she found it more precious than anything she'd ever owned.

Tears flooded her eyes as she struggled for words with a tongue so tangled by joy she could barely force out a coherent syllable.

Nat placed the lantern on her table, the resting spot now high enough to light the whole room instead of just its corner. He, too, seemed surprised by her surroundings, a fact measured out when he spoke.

"I knew they were up to something, but I'd never have guessed something like this."

She gave a strangled laugh, and the tears she'd hoped to control came spilling down her cheeks.

He shook his head. "You'll have to do better than that if you hope to pass as a boy."

The words could have been harsh, but he said them in a joking manner as he used his sleeve to dry her face. "You'll want to obtain a measure of calm before you go meet their curiosity. I suspect the whole crew has gathered to hear of your reaction. They must have planned this between them all to have the supplies brought in and the work done in the short time we were absent."

Sam straightened her tunic and schooled her features into a calm expression before nodding. "And I must go up to give them my thanks. This, more than anything, is a gift I can never repay."

New tears threatened to sprout where Nat had wiped the old ones away, but she brushed the corners of her eyes with her sleeve and managed a shaky smile. "No time better than the present."

Nat collected the lantern as she headed back up the stairs, no longer feeling the weight of her labors much at all. Her muscles were sure to be sore come morning, but she suspected her sleep would be deeper than ever before.

No sooner had she raised her head above the opening than Nat's prediction proved true. All but Mister Garth had gathered near enough to the hatch to hear her when she called out to them.

"Thank you for the change in my circumstances. It means more than you can imagine."

Seamus, who had planted himself barely an arm's length from the opening, shot her a grin. "Weren't much as all that. We've been meaning to gussy up the bilge room for many a voyage now."

She gave him a doubting glance even as another voice came from the gathering shadows to say, "After all, who knows when you'll be ousted so one of us can take up residence in your place."

"Alls we need is the rum barrel, and someone will be more deserving."

"Or maybe we're planning to increase our coffers by taking on passengers now that you've shown a better use for the bilge room."

Teasing comments followed one after the other, laughter and protests in equal measure.

Sam had listened to them often enough since coming from her hiding place to know this meant acceptance of her thanks as well as a need not to make too big a matter of it and risk embarrassing them. She waved a hand toward the sailors she could barely make out and turned back down to where Nat waited with the lantern.

He smothered a yawn, and she took the light from his hand. "You should seek your own hammock. You're as tired as I was." Somehow, Sam doubted she'd be able to sleep just yet with the energy of the crew's welcome humming through her like an aether-driven demand.

Nat mumbled thanks and moved toward the stairs when Sam realized he had not locked her in.

Not wanting to get him in trouble, she called back, "You still need to turn the key."

The distance shaded his features, but his grin came to her bright in contrast to the rest of his face. "The lock was to protect the crew from the worry of an imagined danger. Their efforts here show they see you as so much more than trouble. Go to your rest and don't give a thought to whether you'll be able to meet Jenson for the cinnamon discussion on the morrow if I don't come with the key."

He couldn't see how her expression matched his only because he turned to make his way back to the deck, and most likely, down to the crew quarters.

Sam took the precaution of blowing out the light before crawling into her hammock, a wise decision when she doubted she'd keep her eyes open for the time necessary to snuff it once settled. Not even joy could provide enough energy to counter the return of her exhaustion.

25

N at rose bright and early with the rest to get the ship underway. They had time to make up, and he wasn't the only one eager to see how the repairs withstood the pressures of sea. What brown wood they'd felled proved riddled with insects so they'd had no choice but to fashion the paddles from the purple. Unlike the rest, though, he had no wish for them to reach port any faster.

"Mister Bowden!"

He spun at the sound of Mister Trupt's call, realizing he'd headed for the engine room hatch out of habit. A day or two on the island, and he'd forgotten how he'd been banished from Mister Garth's domain forever.

"Just where do you think you're going?" the first mate asked as soon as Nat reached reasonable earshot.

Nat ducked his head. "I'd forgotten for a moment. I swear I wasn't out to make trouble."

Mister Trupt gave him an all too familiar look at his wording, but left off his standard warning in favor of, "Mister Garth is in a foul mood this morning. He says the paddle repairs are dragging funny and blames the purple wood. For all we know, he might have the right of it, but like as not it's repairs made while afloat, as if we'd had a choice in that."

The first mate stopped and shook his head. "And listen to me blathering on. Seems like the trip to paradise made us all a little soft in the head." He reached out and rubbed Nat's hair.

As much as Nat hated when the first mate, or anyone, did so since it made him feel much younger than his fifteen years, he chose not to protest. Mister Trupt had spoken truly about the island. It seemed to have taken the edge off each and every one of them.

A round of loud, bitter cursing rose from the engine room, and Nat revised his thought. Every one of them who'd gone ashore.

"Don't think of going to lend a hand, Mister Bowden. Whatever assistance you might offer would be undermined by his increased agitation. The man is forever grumbling about one thing or another. No need to give him more cause, especially with the crew all praises for our little stowaway's cooking. As long as the wind blows true, and Sam's contraption holds a steady line, we'll be in a real port and contracting out for real paddle boards soon enough. The repairs need but to hold until then."

Nat didn't bother to answer, the words a dagger in his heart. Even the name the first mate used for Samantha spoke of how soon they'd part ways forever. Every time he heard "Sam," it reminded him of what was to come.

Pushing down his hurt, Nat shrugged. "You'll want me in the rigging then?"

Mister Trupt gave him a sound thump on the back. "Now that's the Bowden boy I know. Always ready to jump in. However, I gave you a charge you're neglecting."

Where Nat expected a scowl, the man laughed. "I happen to know we'll all be enjoying the cinnamon porridge as Sam is already down in the galley with Jenson. They're talking up a storm. I only hope some of their energy goes into the porridge, or spices or not, it'll be burnt to a crisp."

Nat waited for the first mate to finish speaking, the man unusually talkative in the aftermath of their discovery. Still, why shouldn't he be? Thanks to Samantha, they'd weathered storms a plenty, discovered a new island, found goods that should bring a pretty penny, and knew what tack to set without waiting for the stars.

Even Mister Trupt felt the joy when their very cheer meant Nat's sorrow.

He worked to keep his step lively so he didn't stand out quite as much among the crew when on a normal voyage he'd be dancing around his tasks. This time, Nat could have waited another year or more before dropping anchor at the port when he stood to gain as much as any of them.

"'Ware," came the cry from Phil as Nat started up the rigging.

A loose rope end slashed down toward him, and he barely ducked it, oblivious until Phil's call.

"You've gone soft on me," Phil teased as he waited for Nat to bring the rope up to him. "Too much time with your lady."

"She's not my anything."

Nat's tone brought a frown to Phil's brow.

"I didn't mean anything by it," the rigger apologized.

Nat could see both the confusion and curiosity swamping the man, and took a deep breath before waving the apology aside. "I know you didn't. I'm just on edge. Pretty soon we'll be at the port and sending Sam out on her own."

He gave no further explanation. The crew would be happy to see her go. They'd thanked her with changing over her quarters into something not much worse than where the captain laid his head, but it wouldn't last.

Phil's eyes narrowed as he gazed upon Nat for a long, silent moment. "There may be something done about that," he said, half under his breath as he turned away to address the next section of the sail.

Nat had no intention of letting the rigger take him over to the seedier parts of the dock for a distraction. He planned to spend every moment he didn't have responsibilities in helping Sam find a safe place to sleep, and some work where she wouldn't be discovered either for her gender or the deeper secret that made her unable to stay on board longer than necessary. She'd have a nice purse from his share, but it wouldn't last if she didn't find a proper circumstance.

He ignored the hope he'd be able to find her again if they came this way, knowing all too well they'd most likely be returned to the shorter Mediterranean routes after having had as much trouble as they'd experienced in crossing the Atlantic.

26

*J*enson let out a deep laugh as Sam told him yet another story of her sister's lady's maid. The man had a deep appreciation for when those who looked down their noses at others got what was coming to them. Though he hadn't told her why, Sam knew enough to keep to the type of tales he'd enjoy.

Nat had told her to stay on the cook's good side, a direction she'd failed the moment, as a stowaway, she'd taken a portion of food intended for the engineer. She'd been starving, and by the twist of fate, the poor choice had won her Nat's friendship instead of a swim in the deep waters. Still, it had been a lot to make up for even before she flavored the porridge so the crew praised her for taking over Jenson's role.

"You can be a hand in my galley anytime, Sam. I ain't had such a good time in an age, and look, the porridge isn't even burnt."

Sam shot him a grin. "I kept a close eye on it. If anyone would have to suffer the burnt bits, it would be me."

He laughed again, hard enough so tears came to his sun-wrinkled eyes. "Now that's the truth if ever I heard it. And the best reason of all to make this porridge just as tasty as the one you served a small portion of the crew. To hear those men tell it, they're the favored bunch. Does no one any good with some putting on airs."

The way he puffed up his chest and directed a haughty glare at Sam sent her into a fit of giggles he chose to ignore.

"From the smell rising off this pot, we have no worries. Who would have thought shavings from those little sticks could make such a difference? Sure wasn't me. When the captain had such objects sent down to the galley, well, I thought him touched in the head, not that I'd say so to his face, mind you, but the thought was there."

She grabbed the big ladle down from the shelf and handed it to him. "Not sticks. Spices. And when I made it before, I only used the cinnamon, terrified you'd have my head for touching your flavorings. Now we've got nutmeg added in to give it a bite."

Jenson thrust the ladle through his belt and grabbed the pot, waving her off went she went to share the load. "You've done enough showing me there's some of those fancy noble ways as can ease a simple man like myself. Besides, with those short legs of yours, you'd be spilling the porridge all over the below deck. It smells too good to waste."

She didn't try to argue. Nat was a bit taller, but not anywhere near the height of Jenson, and she'd struggled to keep the balance between the two of them the other day. Instead, she collected the bowls. "No need for a second trip this way either."

He grunted a response, already half through the door.

Sam compared this morning with the previous ones on board and smiled.

She wished it could be like this every day—that she could stay here with these men—for all she knew the hope nothing but a flight of fancy. The captain had decided, and she couldn't very well question his thinking. She'd experienced more control on this ship than any other time in her limited existence, but it took just a single weak moment, and she could put the whole vessel and every one of its crew at risk.

Her morose thoughts threatened to swallow up the good mood she'd experienced since waking to an unlocked door, and finding not a single glare or frown as she made her way to the galley. Sure, she knew things would have been different had she crossed paths with the engineer, but she refused to let one sour face destroy her day. Why let her worries do the same?

The decision had little effect until their heads rose above deck level to see the sailors scramble to assemble. If she'd had any doubts as to the reason, the many deep sniffs gave proof enough even without the grins sent her direction.

Remembering Nat's caution, Sam set the stack of bowls next to the pot and stood behind Jenson so it was clear who was the cook and who the helper. She had not been joking when she spoke of getting the burnt bits at the bottom. Sam had observed enough to know the sailors were served first, then the cook and finally his assistants.

She couldn't question the order, either. She'd spent the morning largely sitting and talking with the cook while the others had prepared the ship, climbing ropes and tending to the boards. Besides, had she been offered a bowl, she'd have had to go off to find a place to settle down and eat.

Instead, she handed Jenson the dishes and got to hear appreciative comments in return. The sailors knew the same as Nat and were careful to address Jenson with their generous words, but often enough a wink or grin came winging her way, once again showing how the crew had changed its mind about her. It shouldn't have meant a thing, not when she'd be gone so soon, but it did.

27

$\mathcal{M}$ ister Trupt seemed to have forgotten Nat's responsibility for Sam beyond the one mention in the process of getting back to their voyage. Nat surely wasn't going to remind him when Jenson offered a reasonable substitute and they all benefitted from the pairing.

After he'd lost ground with the crew because of hiding her presence, and all the misunderstandings that went with the choice, finally he had the chance to show nothing much had changed. He proved once again how he wanted to understand every piece of the vessel and wasn't afraid to work for the privilege.

On the rare occasions he had a moment to catch a breath, Nat wondered where Sam had gotten to, but he never questioned her control. She'd proved often enough to him and every member of the crew she had not only the ability to hold herself from dismantling anything but also how she could marshal her knack in their favor.

"Nat, come on down."

He glanced toward the deck to see Phil below, a rare enough occurrence when the man had both eyes open. Worse still it looked as though the whole crew gathered there, those on duty and those supposed to be tucked up in their hammocks.

His confidence in the crew's recovered opinion, and in her control, vanished. He made his way down as directed, hands grown clumsy. Whatever had brought them together, Phil clearly stood as ringleader.

Things had been going too well for it to be mutiny on their minds, which left only Sam as the cause.

"Don't look so nervous," Seamus said when Nat's feet touched the ground. "We're just off to speak with the captain, and we think you should be there."

If anything, this attempt at comfort, especially when delivered with an unusually sober expression, made Nat's stomach roil. They'd been sailing for half a day at this point, too far from the island to turn back without serious cause.

He tried to see Mister Garth in the group, but the steady hum of the engine through the deck boards suggested Sam had not wandered into the engineer's realm.

Nat cursed his inattention. Whatever had brought the crew to this state, especially when even Sam commented on how welcoming they had been, he could not shirk the responsibility. He should not have expected her to stay with the cook.

Mister Trupt and the captain had put her fate in Nat's hands. He'd forgotten the charge, or rather dismissed it when given the chance to return to his former existence. Now he couldn't let her suffer alone.

All this and more rushed through his brain in the short journey from where they'd collected him to the captain's cabin, but he still had no answer to the cause. What had she done that was so unforgivable? He flinched from the possibilities, his burden not just in Sam's defense but also in whatever loss they'd suffered.

"Bring him round," Phil called as the captain swung his door open.

The sailors nudged and pushed Nat through them until he stood right in front of the man he'd failed.

"What is the meaning of this, Mister Bowden?"

Nat stared at the captain, the blood draining from his face.

Then Phil stepped forward, partially shielding him from the captain's presence. "We have a need to discuss with you. It concerns Nat as well, but he doesn't know our purpose."

The captain looked around the group, and his face grew stern. The frown taking hold of his expression looked much different than the one of concentration he normally wore. "And what is this concern that takes all of you from both duties and rest?"

Nat could see Captain Paderwatch's mind spinning with the same questions he held, but could offer no better answers. The captain's gaze narrowed and he sought out Nat, who tried to keep his shoulders firm instead of cowering.

"And where is Miss Samantha?"

Again, Phil took the position as leader. "Not to worry. Sam's busy with Jenson, a perfect time for this."

The captain changed his focus to the rigger, his eyebrows rising. "Is that so? And just who will be keeping us afloat while we have this mysterious discussion?"

A smile cracked Phil's serious demeanor. He let out an earsplitting whistle that caught the attention of everybody on deck, and likely those not present as well. "He's seen us all now. The point is made."

With this curious announcement, the majority of the sailors went back to whatever they'd been doing before this event, leaving only four crew members beyond the captain and Nat.

"So's you know we be of one mind in this. Can't fit us all in your cabin."

The captain made no protest at how the rigger had taken control of the conversation.

"Gentlemen," he said with a nod. "If you'll join me?"

Nat trailed after, desperate to know what this was about even if it meant breaking down the door. But Phil had wanted him present so present he was.

$\mathcal{T}$HE CABIN SEEMED UNCOMFORTABLY CROWDED with the six of them inside. The ship had neither the size nor the number of officers to require a big meeting room, and the table and chairs brought up on deck for rare formal occasions at the captain's table would not have fit within.

"Have a seat, Phil, since you seem to be the one to start this discussion."

The rigger crossed to the chair Nat usually claimed and sat upon it awkwardly. Whatever confidence had driven him this far seemed to vanish in a space so focused on those skills Phil did not share.

The captain seemed to notice this effect as well because he swept his papers onto a side table before taking his seat so they had only a bare cord of wood between them.

"Now what is troubling the crew? I had thought things were going well."

Nat waited for the words to condemn Samantha, and him as well, though why the captain remained unaware of her transgressions he couldn't quite figure.

"Things have been going well, Captain, sir," Phil began, his voice much softer than when up in the ropes. "And, see, we know exactly why that is."

"Oh?"

"Yes, sir," said one of the others.

Nat couldn't see which from where he crouched jammed in a corner. At least they did more than stand silent witness, though Nat was unsure whether he should see this as a benefit or harm.

Phil tried to straighten his lanky form on the chair, then gave up when his head hit the ceiling. "Yes, sir, we know, and we've got a contention with one of your decisions."

Nat could see the captain struggling not to smile at Phil's attempt to mimic formal speech.

Questioning the captain could have serious repercussions, but the lack of tension among the key players let Nat relax just a bit. He leaned forward, more curious than fearful all of a sudden.

"You know the captain's decisions are final." Though Captain Paderwatch stated one of the firmest laws in all the fleet, merchant or naval, he put nothing but idle curiosity in his tone, showing as much interest as Nat felt in the answer.

Despite the captain's calm reaction, Phil seemed to shrink into himself for a moment before he got under control. "Yes, sir. This is no mutiny if that's what you're thinking. You're an odd bird—pardon me for saying so—but you treat us right and bring profits where we were sure to lose out on any other vessel. Just look at us now. Lost at sea, sustaining damage, and with no port in sight. What do you manage but to bring us to an island with its own potential for putting coins in our pockets despite everything."

The captain raised one eyebrow. "While I'm glad to hear you approve, I'm sure Mister Trupt has better uses for your time than to fluff me up."

Phil flushed a bit then and gave a little laugh.

"So, what is it you disagree with? You, and all the rest of the crew."

The rigger dragged in a deep breath, and when he spoke, the words all ran together so rapid did he put forth the contention. "We don't like how's you're planning to cast off the Natural, Captain. She's proven her value more than once when the whole ship was on the line. Those things I said, well, your luck has much to do with it, but it were her hands making the repairs. You know it. We know it. Even Mister Garth knows it as that's half of what's making him grumble. We don't see no purpose in dumping her off where some other crew might discover what she can do. She's our good luck. Our mascot. She belongs with us."

A gasp escaped Nat as he struggled to comprehend what he'd heard. Rather than fearing her once again, the crew had gathered together in secret and decided to keep Sam. Whatever he'd been expecting, even once he determined the discussion was not an accusation, he'd never imagined this.

The captain ran one hand over his mostly bald head. "An interesting proposal, Phil, but not one I can rightly consider. The girl is a person. She's not a mascot and not a good luck charm. She has some unique talents that have served us well, but they are part of her nature, not some miracle from the beyond no matter how they appear. I won't have her life on my head if things go sour, and she can't fix it.

He paused and met each one of their gazes before continuing, "No one can prevent every happening, and we're in a dangerous profession. I won't have you blaming her for the bad just as you're crediting her with everything from fixing the gadgets to putting an island in our way. I've heard you all talking, and superstition is nothing to burden a young girl with. It can break a person."

"She won't fail us," Phil argued, "and we know her now. She's not just a miracle."

Captain Paderwatch put both hands flat on his desk, a signal Nat had seen too many times not to know his mind was made up.

The captain shook his head, but apparently considered the gesture an insufficient answer as he added, "You're a smart man. I understand why the crew chose you to bring this to me. Use the head you were given and think on your life as a sailor. How many men, good men, do you know who got the reputation for being unlucky? Who were on too many ships that ran aground, or had rumors dogging their footsteps until they couldn't find a ship to sail? If the crew turns on her, it isn't as simple as putting her off at the next port. You've seen what happens when she's frightened. You'd be signing her death warrant and maybe ours too. Might as well hang her from the yardarm ourselves."

"Respectfully, sir, I understand your meaning, and you're wrong. Them things that happened to the others, well, they happened because those men, good or not, never found a belonging. Sam's one of the crew, signed on or not. There's not a man among us wouldn't stand by her in a storm."

A slight smile curved one side of the captain's mouth. "Barring Mister Garth, I presume. I noticed his absence from your gathering."

Phil ducked his head for a moment and came up wearing a scowl. "Mister Garth's a smart man, too. He won't buck the men on this. He's known those costs you spoke of."

"I wish I could believe you," Captain Paderwatch said. "I know I'm not alone in regretting what is to come when we reach a port."

Sensing the weakening, Nat jumped to his feet only to curse when his head banged into the low ceiling. "We're landing far south of our intended port, Captain. We'll visit many a one as we make our way back up the American coast before crossing. One port's much the same as any other where Sam is concerned. Can't we try letting her stay? You can observe the crew and decide based on the evidence rather than what you fear."

Again, Captain Paderwatch swept his crown, this time aiming his serious look at Nat as he weighed the argument and found it wanting.

Before he could say as how prolonging the situation would do no one any good, Nat tried another approach he felt sure would appeal. "You could observe her. You could see Sam in action and learn more about what makes a Natural tick. You said yourself how you'd have loved the opportunity before we even knew she existed. Would you deny this chance when fate has dropped it in your lap?"

Phil shot him a grin, but Nat stayed tense as he waited for the captain's decision. He'd tried a desperate ploy with no guarantee of success.

The silence seemed to last an age, and Nat could feel drops of sweat gathering on his forehead only to drip down his face. The close quarters made suffering the heat of the day worse than usual. Normally, the captain left his door wide, but he'd closed them in for this confrontation, perhaps hoping to avoid stiffer penalties should talk have come to mutiny.

Just when Nat thought the captain would wave them out without giving any indication of his decision, Captain Paderwatch cleared his throat.

"You make some compelling arguments, both of you, but this is not a simple question about a barrel of rum or bundle of cloth. Miss Samantha is a person with more at risk than any of us. One ill-spoken word could condemn her faster than a judge's gavel. If she stays with us, her life is in the hands of every single member of this crew. At a port, she has the chance to disappear, to become what she appears to be now. Just another young man looking for work. On a ship, there is nowhere to hide."

Nat stifled his protest. Reminding the captain of her inauspicious beginnings as a stowaway would serve no one.

Another pause, this one shorter but no less painful.

"Gentlemen, I'll think on the idea. I can give you no more than that."

He rose, a signal for the rest of them to do the same. They filed out of the hot space in silence.

Nat had arrived full of dread. He left now trying to hang onto hope.

The captain would tell them of his decision when he came to it—a better answer than the flat rejection he'd offered first—but Nat didn't believe he could tell Sam anything yet. He could think of nothing crueler than to raise her hopes only to have the captain decide against them.

28

C aptain's wanting to see you," Sven said as he poked his head into the kitchen where Jenson taught Sam the proper way to gut a fish for the crew's dinner.

"I'll be right up." Jenson didn't pause as he responded. "Probably wants me to make some new fancy meal from that book of his. He goes over everything with me, then I have to remember it down here with the whole crew gone hungry."

Sam barely stopped from giving him a sympathetic tap on the hand. "I could teach you to read. There's not much time before we get where we're going, but I could get you started with your numbers and letters."

Jenson laughed. "As if I have much need for such stuff. My numbers I know. Have to for buying the supplies. But reading is for them as don't have real work to do. No offense."

She shrugged. Sam missed all the reading she used to do, but now that the crew let her work at their sides, she hadn't had much time she could have read anyway. She didn't figure on the situation changing much once she reached the port even if she could get her hands on a book.

"Ahem."

"Don't be twisting in the wind, Sven. I'll come when I'm ready," Jenson said in response to the unsubtle reminder.

"Here's the thing. It's not you the captain wants to see."

The odd look on Jenson's face would have sparked a laugh if tension hadn't taken hold of Sam, seizing her intestines with a mighty grip.

"I've been here all day. I haven't been up to anything. Jenson can vouch for me." The protest rolled from her tongue before she could hold it back and prompted the cook to give her a comforting pat, or what would have been one if his hand weren't coated in fish scales.

"You want me to come up with you? To put in a good word?"

The offer firmed what spine she had left, and Sam shook her head, pushing to her feet at the same time. "No. I'll go. Maybe he has something for me to look at."

"That's the spirit," Jenson said with a smile. "No need to go borrowing trouble, especially when you've been such a good helper."

She gave him a quick nod as she followed Sven out. The change in the crew's attitude still buoyed her up, and she just needed to focus on them instead of dwelling on all the things that could have gone wrong. She had only to stay on the captain's good side for a short while anyway.

The sight of Nat waiting for her before the open door eased some of the tension Sam couldn't will away. She wouldn't be alone after all.

"There you are," Nat said, catching her hand and pulling her through the door.

If she'd been less in control, she might have flinched at the touch. Something felt off about Nat as if he radiated the same agitation she tried to calm.

Sam didn't have the chance to figure him out. Before she knew it, she stood across the desk from the captain with no mechanical apparatus in sight.

"Have a seat, Miss Samantha."

The captain waved her to the second chair, and she perched there, unsure where to place her hands until she twisted them together in her lap, all effort to hide her nervous tension failing. She'd never had tutors, but she could imagine this was how Henry felt when called to task in the stories he'd told her about his studies. She'd laughed with him in the telling, but it didn't seem so amusing now. Especially not with the captain's use of her full name, though he'd rarely used the shortening he'd been the one to order.

"You are finding your accommodations more comfortable, I suspect."

Though not a question, she nodded. "Yes, absolutely, sir. The crew did a wonderful job of making it into cabin space. Not that I deserve a cabin, but I'm sure you'll find good use for it once I'm gone." She stopped her babbling by force of will, a blush heating her cheeks.

Captain Paderwatch said nothing more for a moment, but before she could squirm under his steady gaze, he added. "It's all to the good then. We may indeed have a use for it sooner rather than later."

Nat squirmed in her stead with this pronouncement, his movements visible in the corner of her eye because he'd dropped to the floor, folding his legs under him.

"Am I in trouble, Captain?" She could contain the question no longer. What other purpose could he wish to speak to her about?

His gaze sharpened. "Should you be?"

Sam almost toppled off the seat from the vigorous head shake she gave. "No, sir. I have not touched anything I wasn't told to. I've been helping with the food. Breakfast, midday, and even dinner. Or I was before you called me here. I haven't changed a thing."

Her voice rose on the last, fear making her suddenly aware of every mechanical device the captain had in his cabin, and they came to no small number. Most were too simple, or too little used, to have gathered enough aether, but still her gift highlighted them as if revealing places she could obtain parts.

The captain put his hands down flat on the empty desk. "So you'd say you're under control."

Sam gulped hard, but she hadn't transformed anything since the pump. "Yes, sir."

He slapped both palms against the desk, making her jump until she saw his wide grin. Confusion overwhelmed her.

"That's just remarkable. You are remarkable. You have no idea how much so. Remarkable." He muttered the last a couple of times beneath his breath before getting himself under control and once again adopting a serious demeanor.

"Do you object to being locked in your room when there's no storm and I can't spare crew to watch over you?"

"Captain!" Nat's protest drowned out anything she might have said, and the captain's attention turned to Nat instead of her for the first time since they'd entered.

"It has not escaped my notice how little care you've taken with your charge, Mister Bowden. You do understand if anything had gone wrong, it would be on your head."

"But you had her locked up to ease the crew's worries, sir. The crew is no longer worried. You saw so yourself. They like Sam. And she's been doing work as crew even though she's not on the register. She's not being any trouble."

The captain nodded, his expression a bit too grim for Sam's liking. "You're correct, and you judged the situation well, but a captain's orders are not subject to question. I trust you understand that much Mister Bowden, despite the current circumstances."

"Yes, sir," Nat all but muttered.

"I don't object," Sam cut in. "About locking the door. I understand why you feel the need for precautions. It's only wise. You've been so generous to me. I see no difficulty in returning the favor by being reasonable."

The captain stared at her for a long while this time, his gaze intent as if he would see to the very center of her and understand her soul much like how she saw into the mechanicals to learn what they wanted to be.

"And would you have any objection to performing such repairs as are given to you? Making use of your unique talents?"

Her confusion returned with force even as she shook her head. "Of course not. I enjoy fixing things." She'd spoken the truth if not the whole truth. They'd all be safer if she had some legitimate mechanicals to work on even if she had to limit herself to repairing any damage. It made fighting the whispered desires so much easier and lessened the chance of a bout.

He brought a leather-bound ledger up onto his desk with a thud. "Well, then. I've been thinking on this half the day and I guess all that remains is for you to sign the register."

Sam stared at the list of names, glanced at Nat to find him grinning, then looked back at the book, unsure what he meant.

The captain dipped his pen and placed it in her lax hand. He pointed to the blank space at the end of the list. "Right here, if you please. And as Sam not Samantha. The fewer questions raised the better. You're an extra cabin boy I picked up on the journey. What with Mister Bowden so busy learning the ways of the ship, I have need of someone to tend to his duties."

He winked at her, the expression so unexpected, she just stared at him until a drip of ink fell from the nib to stain the page.

"You can write your name, can you not? If you cannot, an 'x' will serve as you might have noticed. I'll write it in for you."

Sam pushed aside her hesitation as the meaning of this came to her. Before he could change his mind, she signed with a flourish, the tail of her "m" curving into the start of an "a" before she remembered her name had become Sam. She scratched out the extra until only the first three letters were clear then added her last name.

The captain smiled at the sight of her careful hand, but said nothing beyond, "Welcome aboard, Sam Crill."

"This means I'm a member of the crew, yes?"

"Yes."

"Yes, yes!" said Nat, jumping up to grab both her hands. "It means you don't have to make your way among strangers. We won't put you off. The crew wants you to stay, and the captain has agreed. You're one of us now."

Even so, it didn't quite sink in until she saw the amusement on the captain's face.

"Perhaps you could take your celebration to where there's a bit more space, Mister Bowden? And though they've made every effort to stay beyond the door, I suspect you'll find a goodly crowd gathered beyond to join in."

Still dazed, Sam let Nat pull her from the cabin to find the captain had spoken truly as many of the sailors stood not far from the opening, ready to congratulate her.

"And Sam, I expect you in my cabin bright and early to-morrow. We have much work to do," the captain called after them.

"Yes, sir," Sam said, putting all the enthusiasm she could muster into the simple acknowledgment.

She glanced from smiling face to smiling face, amazed and overwhelmed. They'd chosen her. Even knowing what she was, and what she could do, they accepted the risks and want-ed her to stay.

Her back sore from all the pats and her shoulder numb from cheerful punches, Sam stumbled through the gathering, laughter on her lips and tears threatening her eyes.

"I have to go tell Jenson," she said after a bit. "I'll have time to teach him to read after all."

A collective groan sounded from the sailors, and Nat laughed at her. "You'll find no joy in schooling these louts, Sam Crill. There's not a one of them who would prefer the written word to a well-told tale. Besides, you won't have much time for it, not with your new status. The captain has plans to study you."

She pulled up short, nervous once again, but Nat shook his head.

"Don't worry. He means simply to question you about eve-ry aspect of your life until your head aches and your mind is whirling. Nothing you can't handle."

The sailors laughed with him, and after a moment, she joined in as well.

Some part of her even looked forward to the examinations. After all, she'd thought her knack completely wild until neces-sity made her have to use it on purpose and with a goal in mind beyond the wants of the mechanicals themselves. What more could she learn under the tutelage of a true scholar as the crew liked to remember the captain had been?

"Off you go to Jenson. Tell the captain we'd like you to keep your time in the galley if it means more cinnamon porridge though," Phil said, nudging her toward the main hatch.

Sam crossed the open space with a bounce to her step only to falter as her gaze met that of Mister Garth's.

The engineer's glare was enough to make her stumble, but he turned aside to stomp off to the engine room without a word. Sam continued down the steps, trying to recapture her joy so she could tell the cook without a hint of the doubts she now felt in her tone.

29

C aptain Paderwatch called them all together at the evening change of the watch, a rare event, but what he had to say he apparently wanted every one of them to be present for. Nat worried they'd gone astray once more until he saw how the captain's eyes seemed to glitter with excitement despite his stern expression.

"Mister Trupt, if you please."

Nat heard the request because he stood nearby with Sam, the gathered men, and one girl, having broken into smaller groups to share their speculations about the meeting.

The first mate jerked the bell string once, twice, and then a third time as the gathered sailors failed to quiet down.

Finally, only the slush of the hull as it cut through the water, the creak of the paddles, and the rattle of ropes as they slapped the mast remained.

The captain cleared his throat. "Some of you came to me in the crew's name with a proposition I found unusual to say the least. I promised your ringleaders to consider the request, and consider it I have."

A low grumble came from the sailors who'd just risen from their hammocks as the afternoon's events had not spread far enough. Nat feared the mutiny he'd worried about from the start, but then the captain let his smile show.

"I had a discussion with Miss Samantha this evening as some of you know, and my concerns are alleviated."

His announcement met with silence. Whatever they'd been expecting, this hadn't fulfilled their hopes, or perhaps his fancy wording offered no answers at all.

The captain raised both hands as though conducting the sailors' emotions. "The young lady has signed the register. We have a new cabin boy aboard. Gentlemen, meet Sam."

Nat gave Sam a hard shove, and she stumbled into the open space on the quarterdeck.

The crew burst out in cheers, leaving no doubt as to their welcome.

"Out of my way," came a fierce demand as Mister Garth shoved through to the front. "Captain, she's no cabin boy. She isn't even a boy. And what she is could have us on the bottom of the ocean faster than you can thank Your Majesty. She's a Natural," he added as if they weren't aware of her abilities.

While Mister Garth softened his tone somewhat, it still came across as the rejection the man intended, and Captain Paderwatch glared down at the engineer.

Nat wondered if they'd have need for the bilge room's traditional purpose after all.

"Shut your mouth," one of the sailors cried.

"She's a member of the crew. You heard the captain."

Other calls were less polite, and even in the flicker of lantern light, Nat could see her pale skin darken with their language.

He sighed, relieved she wouldn't have to make her way among the lower classes as a boy. A reaction like that would be hard to control, and harder still to live down.

"Gentlemen. Gentlemen."

The captain's voice had no impact on the sailors, who seemed to be gearing up to attack the engineer.

"Stand down!" The shout came from Mister Trupt with enough force to freeze every one of them, Nat and Sam included.

Mister Garth took a step back from the first mate then stepped forward again just as quickly when his movement put him within reach of the nearest crewman.

"Gentlemen," the captain said again, casting a stern gaze over the assembly. "Mister Garth may have broached the topic poorly, but he told only the truth as we all know it. Sam, bearing the title of cabin boy or not, is neither boy nor a sailor. She possesses skills hitherto unknown beyond wild tales, each with more than a grain of truth to them. While she's shown an excess of control..." He paused to give her an appreciative nod. "...many of us have seen what happens when she loses that control with our own eyes."

"It was before she became one of us," a voice called out of the darkness. "She has nothing to fear."

Again the captain raised his hands, though this time he lowered them just as quickly, calling for silence. "I will not risk this ship, nor any of you, in such a foolhardy choice."

"So she's not staying then?" Mister Garth asked in a smug tone.

Captain Paderwatch shook his head. "Oh, she's staying all right. She's signed the register. I'm now accountable for her wellbeing as much as any of you just as she gets a cut of the profits."

He paused as if expecting a protest, but the crew seemed to have already considered such a consequence. Nat thought it only fitting. Without Sam, there would have been no profits and perhaps no ship to reach the harbor.

The engineer's scowl cut deep lines in his face as the lantern shone down on him, but he knew enough to keep silent.

"Sam will not be housed with the crew. The cabin *boy* will remain in the bilge room." Again he paused. "And when not under Mister Bowden's careful eye, that door will be locked."

The sailors burst into a roar of protests, the noise so loud Nat struggled to make out any single statement.

This time Sam raised her arms, waving both hands high above her head until word passed, and they let her speak. "This is my choice. I can't tell you how much I appreciate your coming to my defense. Your welcome means everything to me. But the captain and engineer are right to be cautious. I will not chance losing your good will, or worse, risking any of you."

Jenson shouldered his way to the front, stopping long enough to glare at Mister Garth on his way. "How's Sam to work in the kitchen then? Seems wasteful Nat hanging about when there's other work to be done."

The captain gave the cook a faint smile. "Sam will be under observation at all times, for her own safety as much as ours. She doesn't know her way around a sailing ship and could end up overboard. While Mister Bowden will not be the only one to monitor Sam, the responsibility for knowing where she is and whom she is with will be on his shoulders. Is this understood?"

Jenson thought about it for a moment then nodded, happier now that he'd kept the right to her efforts.

Nat stepped forward as well. "Understood, sir." He suspected Sam would spend more time with the captain than any other.

"Mister Garth?"

The engineer snapped upright as the captain said his name, his scowl still firmly in place. "Understood," he grumbled.

By a silent signal, the sailors started to disperse, heading to their duties or hammocks as if the meeting had not occurred.

"One more thing," the captain called out, bringing them round to face him again. "No one is to speak of this. Sam's abilities are a ship secret. Anyone"—he shot a glare at Mister Garth—"who speaks of it will be dismissed without recommendation."

The engineer's shoulders slumped, and his skin seemed to darken, but he said nothing more.

"And that, gentlemen, is everything I had to say. Get to your duties and to your rest. Mister Bowden, you have charge of our new crew member. See to it Sam is safely tucked in for the night."

Nat gave an acknowledging nod, but his attention stayed on the engineer.

In a weak moment after downing a ration of heavy spirits, Mister Garth had revealed just how he came to be on Captain Paderwatch's vessel. He owed the captain everything as he'd come to the ship with no recommendation and the rumor of passing off another man's work as his. Revealing Sam would cost the engineer any chance at a merchant ship, but Nat still didn't trust the man.

Mister Garth had taken a personal exception to Sam. Such dislike as that didn't go away because of the captain's say so.

Out of the corner of his eye, he saw her bring a hand up to smother a yawn. She'd worked hard all day on top of the excitement both when the captain examined her and this. He doubted she'd even notice being locked in. He had his orders, though, and he had the feeling Sam would be the first to condemn him if he failed to follow them a second time.

They made their way across the deck to the short stairs down into the bilge, his mind only partially on what he was doing. The best way to ensure her safety would be to earn back Mister Garth's good will between now and when they dropped anchor in the Americas. As much as he wished he could approach such a happenstance with confidence, he wondered just how he could accomplish the change when the engineer had as many if not more reasons to stand against him as he ever had for Sam.

30

S am woke to the sound of a knock and a call through the door. A moment later, the key turned. She pulled the blanket tighter around her as Nat came in with a lantern and a bucket.

"I brought you some scrub water. Cabin boy or not, you shouldn't be washing up on deck with the rest of us."

A blush heated her cheeks, but Sam ignored it. "I'm the cabin boy, not you. It's my job to fetch and carry."

"So quick to take my tasks from me?" Nat said with a laugh. "Don't worry. I can get used to having an apprentice of my own."

He turned his back, a signal for Sam to jump up and get ready.

"You're to be my shadow, doing the work I'm doing, unless specifically assigned elsewhere. The captain wants you settled before he starts in on examining you."

She dropped the shirt she'd chosen into the water, and a curse came from her lips that would have turned her sister Lily blue with horror.

Nat spun around, and Sam barely had time to press the damp cloth against her.

"I'm fine," she told him, willing him to face the door again.

After a searching gaze, he returned to his previous position, giving her the chance to root around in the remaining clothing for another shirt to wear while this one dried. She'd been excessively lucky as most sailors had no more than a single shirt to their names. But then Nat came from the same stock as Henry.

"You needn't fear the captain. He won't be harsh," Nat said with more perception than she'd expected of him. "He wants to learn about your Natural abilities. He's a scholar at heart, and you pose a puzzle that would overwhelm any of his nature."

She'd suspected as much once she thought of it though she'd hoped to work with the sailors. She couldn't resist a tease as she stepped into the trousers Nat had given her then joined him at the door. "One of his nature, or yours? You've been quizzing me since you first learned what I could do."

He blew out the lantern to preserve oil and headed toward the faint dawn light visible from the hatch. She wondered if he would answer, but at the last moment, he glanced over his shoulder and said, "If you thought I had questions, you've no experience being under the sharp gaze of one like the captain. You may have taken my duties, but with them you've freed me from endless studies."

Sam perked up at that.

She'd never had the chance to learn from a real teacher, though Lily had taught her to read and Henry gave her access to the whole of his library. She could suffer some prodding queries if she got to ask some of her own. It almost made up for missing out on the ship work.

The morning passed in a rush from one task to the next, proving her fears of being confined in a hot cabin all day to be false.

Nat showed her how to hook her feet so she could check the sails for wear and tear. They worked on weaving some new ropes to replace ones that had started to fray. They even laughed over the thought of her sister seeing Sam's rough stitches repair a split in one of the spare sails.

For once her efforts did not look out of place.

Sam enjoyed every minute of it, knowing she'd found a place where she could be accepted for who she was, not hated for what they feared she'd do.

Every minute, that was, except when she glanced up to see Mister Garth coming out of the engine room hatch. She missed the murmurs of the engine and the gears moving relentlessly as they turned the paddles and sent the ship forward.

As though preternaturally aware of her, the engineer pivoted until he faced her with a fierce scowl twisting his features. The rest of the crew may have accepted her, but Mister Garth showed no sign of softening.

"Take no notice of the man," Phil said as he bunched up the sail and tossed another section in need of repair toward her. "He doesn't like anyone."

Sam tried to take the rigger's words to heart, but the engineer's dislike seemed stronger for her than any other, or maybe it only seemed that way because he stood between her and the engine room where she longed to be.

31

Nat delivered Sam into the galley where she would help Jenson prepare the midday meal. He felt odd without her at his side after a long morning of teaching her how to keep the ship in working condition. She'd proven as eager a cabin boy as he had been when first put on board, joyfully tackling whatever tasks came their way.

In just one morning, she'd been over almost the whole vessel, omitting the captain's cabin and the crew quarters, along with the engine room, of course.

The last thought made him pause while coming up from the galley.

Phil had dismissed Mister Garth's animosity, but Nat could not be as quick to ignore the danger from that quarter. The crew had asked for her to stay, hoping to keep the benefits of her nature while controlling the rest, but Nat knew all too well how little their wishes would matter if ever the captain was faced with a choice between Mister Garth and Sam. The ship needed an engineer if they were to compete with full steam ships bearing the newer engines. They would last without a Natural.

Nat checked for the first mate before popping up on deck and striding for the engine hatch. His lies on top of Mister Garth's history, especially when the man had just started to accept him, made things worse for Sam. He refused to let his choices harm her and didn't want the situation to fester in his own mind either. The engineer deserved his apology at the very least, a small step in the direction of repairing the conflict.

Nat failed to consider the consequences if Mister Garth was not within until after the hatch closed over his head. He should have checked first, but feared the engineer would eject him apology unspoken if he called down. No choice remained but to go forth on the assumption Mister Garth was deeper in the engine room. Worse would be getting caught leaving without trying to speak as it would look suspicious and so undermine the very thing he hoped to accomplish.

The engine room sounded louder than Nat remembered it, the air thick with moisture and the engine struggling against the added pressure. Even the creak of his feet on the steps did not bring the engineer forward, but with the additional cacophony, Mister Garth would be unlikely to notice him unless he stamped hard, something that would only irritate.

Still, Nat came to a halt at the bottom, venturing no further without an invitation.

"Mister Garth," he called. "Are you here?"

A clang followed by a loud curse sounded from the depths of the room.

A moment later, the engineer squirmed out from between two pipes and into the open section of the space. He rubbed his forehead, a clear indication of what had happened in the tighter parts of the room.

"What is it?"

The question came out before Mister Garth's eyes adjusted to the differences in light, or so Nat assumed, because the engineer's expression went from grumpy to downright hostile at the sight of him.

"What are you doing in my engine room?" he bellowed. "Didn't Mister Trupt make it clear you are not welcome in here? Not now, not ever. Don't go expecting me to soften toward you or your creature. The crew might think her some sort of pet, but you don't let a Natural on your ship any more than you'd let a wolf bed down next to your hammock."

Nat took a step back, his heel hitting the lowest step. "I came to apologize. I understand why you feel the way you do, and I deserve your wrath. I did what I did with good cause, but you gave me your trust—"

"And you trampled it into the dirt. I know exactly what the worth of a nobleman's apology is." He spat close enough for Nat to feel the spray on his bare toes. "Just because the captain sees that thing as yet another machine to explore like all the other gadgets he picks up wherever we go, and just because the superstitious crew thinks she'll protect them from any storm, I'm not fooled."

He stamped his foot against the boards. "She has no place on this ship, and I'm not likely to pretend otherwise just so you can feel comforted. Now get back on deck where you belong, *cabin boy*. And leave me to my work. The girl's coming nowhere near my engine with her magical hands and twisty ways. Do you hear me?"

The engineer had come so close, Nat half-reclined on the steps to avoid being knocked over. Still, he refused to let the other man intimidate him, especially when he'd heard something in Mister Garth's voice that led him to understand why the engineer was so adamant in his opposition a little better.

When Mister Garth straightened, so did Nat. "She can't do what you do, Mister Garth. She hears what things want to be, or what they were but are no longer. She can't maintain a working engine. It takes training. It takes an engineer."

"You think I don't know that?" The engineer practically spat the words, foam spraying from between his lips. "I don't need some book-learned fancy boy to tell me how to do my job any more than some wild Natural. And I certainly don't need any pity from one neither. I know exactly what's behind those pretty words of yours. I've been burned twice now. More fool me. I'll not be giving in one more time. Not me." He advanced on Nat, fists raised. "Now get out of my engine room. If you come down here again I'll beat the lights out of you. Go."

Nat scrambled backwards up the steps and out of the hatch faster than he would have thought possible, the engineer's enraged face imprinted on the back of his eyes.

A hand clamped on Nat's shoulder before he could regain his feet. "Did I not make myself clear, Mister Bowden?"

The vision before him now offered no more comfort as Mister Trupt scowled down at Nat.

"You are not to bother the engineer, not to interfere with his workings, and not to enter the engine room for any cause no matter what. Is that understood?"

"I just wanted to apologize," Nat said, his voice wavering more than he would have preferred. "I wanted to end the bad blood between us and make the ship mood better."

Mister Trupt shook his head. "And you think something as simple as words can fix what you've done? It seems you're too ready with more than just your swears." The first mate's expression softened. "You've broken his trust, a trust given grudgingly in the first place. It'll take more than words to repair the betrayal, if it can even be repaired. A man's only as good as his word."

When Nat went to protest, Mister Trupt raised one hand and his eyes hardened. "It doesn't matter the reason. It matters the choice. You risked the crew, the ship, and his precious engine for reasons you knew but chose not to share, making the decision for all of us. The crew may have decided to adopt Sam, but it doesn't change what you did. You have to live with your decision—and the consequences from it—just as the rest of us do."

Nat slumped, hearing the truth in the first mate's speech for all he wanted to deny it. Had he revealed Sam when he'd first found her, things would have turned out much different, worse perhaps rather than better, but he would not have violated the trust put on him by the captain, Mister Trupt, the crew, and especially the engineer.

Mister Trupt thrust a hand down to help Nat to his feet. "Don't dwell on the past, Mister Bowden. The time has gone, and nothing you do can change it. Look rather to the future and let your failings before inform how you go on. I can't promise Mister Garth will soften."

A frown marred his features. "I'd be surprised to see him do so to be honest, but I can speak for the rest of us. You're a good boy if young and undisciplined at times. But your heart's in the right place. Now if only you can convince your head to follow. You are not to bother the engineer again."

"Yes, sir," Nat muttered, still feeling the bite of the first mate's scolding.

"Now get back to work. There's no slacking with me on deck as you well know it."

Nat didn't need to be told twice. He scanned the ship for what needed to be done and joined Sven in scrubbing the deck clear of a slippery moss that was quick to take hold in this damp climate. The grueling labor, especially under this heat, seemed appropriate penance for his poor judgment first when discovering Sam stowed away and then again just now in confronting the engineer. He had much to make up for.

32

S am carried a stack of bowls up to the deck for the midday meal and helped Jenson with the queue as she had the previous morning. She'd learned very little of a sailor's time was wasted, but she couldn't complain. Swapping stories with Jenson brought her back to cheerful times in Henry's kitchen, and knowing she provided necessary help strengthened her whenever exhaustion threatened.

Still, when Jenson took the bowl from her hand, spooned a generous serving of stew into it, and handed it back, Sam didn't reject the offer.

"I've served many a meal on my own. Why don't you go find Mister Bowden and catch up?"

Sam ducked to hide the heat coloring her cheeks. She'd figured out the crew thought they had some kind of a romance growing between them and no amount of protests would sway the sailors.

"Thank you," she mumbled as she scanned for Nat.

When she found him, though, he sat all alone, something she hadn't seen since being allowed to share meals with the crew. She wasn't sure whether he wanted her company.

Nat glanced up then and caught her eye, his mouth twisting into a rueful expression.

She wondered what it meant and Sam had no other recourse but to join him if she were to find out.

"Come to share in my purgatory?" Nat said when she came near enough. "I can't promise much conversation."

Sam sank to the deck, mimicking the way he folded his legs under him. "What changed since I saw you last?" She almost added a tease, the sailors having rubbed off on her a little too well, but controlled the instinct.

He shrugged. "I tried to push an apology on Mister Garth. To say it went poorly would be understating the case. Mister Trupt has barred me from the engine room without express invitation, and I'm not to approach the engineer for any reason at all."

Sam patted Nat on the shoulder twice before withdrawing her hand, awkward in the knowledge many watched them for some proof of affection.

She cared for him, but not in the way the crew expected. He had become her best friend.

Nat shrugged again. "It's not anything I don't deserve. I didn't think it through. I just didn't want the captain to have to decide between the two of you."

"Between us?" A stab of panic hit Sam in the chest. What captain would choose a Natural, no matter how much in control, over his engineer?

This time Nat offered the comforting pat. "It won't come to that. The crew is behind you, and Mister Garth seems to have settled for keeping his domain free of us. I'd hoped for more, but I have only myself to blame."

"You have me. To blame, I mean. If I hadn't been there, none of this would have happened in the first place."

That brought a smile to his face, though she'd not intended the reaction.

"You're right. I would never have seen the engine room at all. I'd never have made such a wonderful friend. Most likely we'd never have survived the first storm in order to meet the second, and if we had, we'd have been lost at sea with faulty charts to guide us."

She didn't know what to say, so returned his smile and bent to her meal.

They ate in silence, but unlike the uncomfortable solitude Nat had been enduring before she came, Sam thought this felt companionable. They'd grown so familiar with each other's company they didn't need to fill the air with chatter.

"Captain says you're to go to his cabin after the dishes," Nat announced when she'd thought he would say nothing until they were done.

She didn't know how to react. Part of her dreaded the pressure of being alone with the captain in a room filled with gadgets of all shapes and sizes. The rest of her looked forward to whatever challenges he would set to her.

"What do you think he'll want to teach me? Jenson says he teaches you charts and such, but mostly about the places he's been and people he's met there. Jenson says the captain has been all over the world."

Nat turned to look at her and started laughing, his early gloom having vanished. Or rather, it was in the process of transferring to Sam, who lowered her empty bowl to the boards with a thud.

He reacted to her scowl with a weak attempt to control his laughter, and she waited impatiently for him to stop chortling.

"And just what is so funny about what Jenson told me? He might stretch the truth here and there in the name of a tale, but I don't see why he would in this case."

Nat swallowed hard enough for his Adam's apple to bounce visibly. He raised a hand to ask for a moment, then said, "Sorry. No, the cook told you the truth. It's more your expression." He paused to laugh once more. "Any other on this ship would curse the sorry fate that dropped him into the captain's way, and have many a time. I took to the ropes to get away from his lectures. But here you are, all starry eyed and cheerfully contemplating hours of words you'll never have a need for."

"Oh." Sam glared at him. "You've got the head for learning, but it was always handed to you. I'll bet you had tutors from a young age. All I ever had was books, and few enough of them before Henry. I wish I'd had enough of a chance that I'd scorn it now."

He sobered then. "I'm sorry. You're right. It's nothing to laugh about. The crew doesn't want learning so of course they scorn it. They don't see the value in it. Honestly, I don't see the value in as much detail as I've gotten from the captain, but some of it is interesting. You'll see, I suspect."

If Sam hadn't been still glaring at him, she'd have missed the way he tensed after saying the last. "What?" she demanded.

A grimace drew down the corners of his mouth. "Nothing. It's just you may not find the captain teaching as much as prying into what makes you tick. He aims to understand how you, of all the Naturals, can function in society. In anyone else, it would be considered intrusive curiosity. In him, it's scholarship."

"Oh," she said again.

The thought of being poked and prodded much like how she worked on mechanicals had less appeal than learning about new places, especially since she knew there were havens where Naturals lived together, so she couldn't be unique as all that. But she couldn't go telling the captain, not without risking the safety of all those who sheltered there.

"Well, I suppose he earned the right," she said after a moment. "After all, without his agreement, I'd be cast off on the nearest port with no one to help me."

Nat pushed to his feet, the dirty bowl in one hand. "He's not a bad man. He'll treat you well. It's just, intentions aside, he can get carried away. You'll be fine, and perhaps you'll enjoy the process. It's a bit like what you said with the mechanicals, I suppose, only it's your gears and springs he'll be holding up to the light."

She gave a soft laugh and joined him as they headed off to the wash bucket where the crew deposited their dirties. Whatever the captain might demand of her, it couldn't be worse than contemplating whether or not she could catch a rat before she grew too weak to survive.

$\mathcal{N}$AT HELPED SAM WITH THE dishes, so before she knew it, the time to go to the captain's cabin had arrived. She tried to school her expression as they approached, but her nerves kept twitching, and no matter how much she concentrated on all the good things Nat had said about the captain, her palms were slick and her fingers trembling by the time Nat rapped on the door.

"Is that you, Mister Bowden?" came a cheerful voice from within. "Come in, both of you."

The captain opened the door as he said the last, wiping his forehead with a cloth. Though the portholes were open, with the closed door, it had grown rather stuffy, or perhaps it was always this way.

The whispers from many devices tucked throughout the cabin distracted her from the muggy heat as the captain spoke again.

"I'll have command of her through the rest of the day until evening, I suspect. You're free to go about your duties. We have much to discover."

The way he rubbed his hands together, matched with the wide grin stretching his cheeks, made Sam squirm a little. She tossed a nervous glance to Nat, but he only smiled back and gave her a reassuring nod, or rather one intended to be reassuring. Since it also served as a goodbye, she didn't feel comforted in the least.

Once Nat stepped over the threshold, the captain said, "Close the door after you if you please, Mister Bowden. We have no intention of distracting the crew."

Sam's gut clenched even before the door sealed with a quiet thud. Just what would they be doing that he thought it would attract attention from the busy sailors beyond the door?

"Have a seat, Miss Samantha, and we'll get started if you please. There's so much to explore, I almost don't know where to begin."

She rubbed her hands against the trouser legs to dry them as the captain backed further into the room and moved to go around his desk. The effort to calm herself proved a waste as she saw what his position had obscured before.

There on the flat surface lay a half-dismantled gadget. Its demands added to the murmur she always experienced when in this space. As though it recognized her presence as well, the object cried out for her to repair, replace, and improve whatever it had been into something better and much different.

Her hands curled into fists tight enough so her ragged nails bit deep into her palms, but even the pain could not distract her.

She'd thought nothing worse than contemplating raw rat for dinner, but she'd been wrong. How would she be able to prove herself under control when she could barely think over the blood pounding through her temples and the aether-driven demands? If he'd wanted to test her control by putting this within reach and denying it to her, he'd found the right test—and she feared she'd already failed.

33

C ome along now. I thought you'd be eager to show me how it's done," the captain said when she failed to move forward.

Sam stared at him for a moment. "You want me to fix it?"

He gave her a sober look. "You believed this some kind of punishment, did you? I thought Nat would have given you some idea of what to expect...of this meeting and of me."

Sinking onto the chair bought her a moment to control her expression, not that it mattered when he'd already seen through to her fears.

The captain lifted her chin with one finger, forcing Sam to meet his gaze. "Mister Bowden told me about how you discovered the broken pump when Mister Garth thought to show your true nature. He said mechanical objects spoke to you in some way. Is this true?"

She could only nod.

Captain Paderwatch shook his head. "What a life you must have led to expect such treatment from a scholar like myself. Though I suppose being labeled a dangerous fugitive from birth didn't help your perception of others."

"It wasn't from birth."

She hadn't meant to say anything, but the correction burst forth before she could stop it.

"Hmm, I suppose not. How would they know one way or the other when you could barely get your fist into your mouth?"

Sam shook her head. "It wasn't that. I didn't start to hear mechanicals until later. I don't know how old I was, but it was after Mother died."

The captain reached across the desk to take her hand, unmindful of how his sleeve caught on one of the gears and threw it far from its fellows. "There now, you poor girl. Raised by your father were you? That explains a lot."

She didn't want to offend, but his pity made her feel as if she were denying Lily's presence in her life. "I had my sister. And my father didn't live much longer. But it isn't her fault or his how I turned out. They did their best."

He withdrew then, his mouth lowering into a frown. "I didn't mean to imply any different. Of course they did nothing wrong. I'm sure they both tried their level best. A weaker or less caring pair would have turned you in as the law demands. As to bringing about your nature, if a cause was known, Naturals would be extinct, driven out by all those who fear them. Care or lack of it has nothing to do with the knack you possess."

She had meant they were not responsible for how she'd turned out so boyish, not whatever made the mechanicals able to communicate, but this time Sam let the comment pass, too distracted by yet another gear cast away with his movement. Much longer on his desk and this object would become nothing more than a scatter of parts, losing even the fragment of aether that clung to it much like Nat's rock had done when pried from its resting place.

Her hand crept into her pocket to find Nat's very rock. Touching its surface helped calm her and softened the pull from the broken machine though nothing beyond scattering the pieces or giving in to it could quiet the call.

"You've not heard a word I said, have you, Miss Samantha? I told you I did not intend to torment, but I suppose I've done exactly that with my carrying on. Nat always said I could make a lecture out of a single word if given half a chance…or at least he did before he came under my command. He has too much respect for the office to speak in such a way."

Eased by Nat's imprint on the rock, Sam allowed a smile to escape as the captain proved his words in the easiest way possible.

He rubbed a hand over his balding pate. "I'm doing it again, aren't I? And you're too polite to say a thing. Here's what I want of you: take this machine I purchased in Italy. It's never worked, and I can't remember for the life of me what it was supposed to do in the first place. I can think of no better tool for our purposes. No one will mourn it, and I, for one, will delight in whatever you come up with."

A sudden flare of aether longing made it difficult to follow his words, but what he'd said could not have been what he meant.

Sam swallowed against the pressure to reach just a little further and snag the gear he'd dropped from his sleeve, but she couldn't keep her gaze from clinging to the thin circlet of metal.

"You want me to change this? To follow its demands?"

The captain's face split into an almost boyish grin as he brought his hands together. "Exactly. And I want you to tell me what you're doing every step of the way. What you feel, and how it communicates with you."

"Exactly." She repeated the word, still not quite able to believe it. But the aether wouldn't let her delay any longer. She didn't know if she'd be able to do as he asked. She'd rarely been able to communicate when tracing the lines of aether. She'd managed with Nat, though, so perhaps she could now if she tried hard enough.

Her last bit of resistance disappeared. The lone gear fell prey to her questing fingers, leaping into her grasp as if just as eager, and she supposed it was.

Remembering his request, Sam forced back the fog and pushed words from between her lips. "You're hurting it. This has been broken for so long, it doesn't have much aether to claim, and when you draw its pieces apart, you're hurting it."

She hadn't meant her first information to take the shape of a scold, but once the words formed, it became easier than she'd expected to speak them.

"Oh." His quiet exclamation was coupled by a quick action. He swept up the pieces and shoved them toward her in a jumbled mess.

They resembled little more than a trash heap now, but Sam could feel the aether strengthening, shored up by each piece touching another.

"That's better. They're happier now."

He leaned forward until his exhale blew a breeze across her cheek. "They? It's a collective rather than pieces of a whole? Fascinating."

Sam felt her brow crease as she tried to understand what he meant by those words. He didn't seem to expect a reply, though, and he'd asked her to find the purpose in what barely had the awareness to speak to her.

She tried when trying went against everything she'd trained herself to do, but the mechanism had been broken for too long. The captain hadn't cared enough to imbue it with something of himself. More likely, it had lain broken all this time tucked on a shelf and forgotten.

After stirring the gears, picking one up then another, brushing her fingers against the part that still had some structure and nudging the loose gears against it several times, Sam sat back, despair eating at her.

"I can't."

Her words came out so softly the captain had to lean even closer to hear them until his face almost pushed against hers.

The eager expression he wore conflicted with her results so harshly Sam pushed up from the chair with a cry, needing to escape.

The captain caught her arm. "What's wrong? What upset you?"

It was the last question, the concern for her over the failure she'd proved to be that made Sam hesitate instead of jerking free.

When she looked at him again, the eagerness had stripped away, a furrowed brow and frown taking its place.

Sam's shoulders slumped. "I can't do it. I can't fix the mechanism."

He shook his head. "I didn't say for you to fix it. I understand from Nat, and what little I know of Naturals, the way something had been is not necessarily the way it will end up. I've given you my permission to do whatever you will with it."

She fisted her hands at her sides. "That's what I'm saying. I can't. I can't fix it or recreate it or do anything with it. It doesn't want to be anything at all."

The captain let her go, but Sam had lost the will to escape. She slouched back onto the chair and stared at the pieces.

If they'd mocked her for her failure, she would have felt better than this. To feel nothing, to have no connection, left a hollow in her soul, as though whatever made her a Natural had just as easily slipped away.

"So tell me, Miss Samantha. Tell me what makes this machine any different than the rest."

His request irritated her, poking her out of the grief. "Maybe I'm the one who's broken. Maybe whatever knack I had vanished when I denied first the engine then everything else. I've never tried to fix things before unless that's what they wanted. I listened to the aether, and it told me what to do. But on this ship, you needed things to be what they were and didn't want to risk any enhancements."

"Very interesting. So the mechanical objects actually direct you?"

The scratch of nib against paper made her glance up so she could scowl at the captain.

"Not anymore." She pushed at the offending collection of parts and watched as three gears took to rolling hard enough they dropped out of sight behind the desk.

He caught her irritation then, but his response was less than comforting as he smiled. "Not five minutes ago you were telling me how I was hurting the pieces. Whatever you are experiencing at this moment, the world of metal machines still talks to you. Whether you crave it or scorn it, your knack has not deserted you."

She dropped her gaze to the table only to flinch as she took in the scattering she, herself, had done. "How can you be so sure?"

His fingers rapped out a pattern on the desktop as he thought, thrumming through the order from pinky to pointer again and again until she wanted to slap her palm over them. But she'd done enough for one day and so kept her violent tendencies under control.

"Hmm," he said after a period much too long for Sam's taste. "Would you be willing to try an experiment? It might seem like the torture you suspected me of at first, but it will prove, I believe, whether your knack is gone for good or whether the issue lies with what I gave you more than you yourself."

Sam shrugged, no longer interested in any experiment. Would the sailors want her if she couldn't offer hope in their darkest hour? Would they cast her out after all?

A rustle of cloth barely broke through her glum thoughts, but a moment later, she jerked her head up, clenching both fists to keep her hands from laying claim to the pocket watch the captain held suspended from a watch chain.

He laughed softly, the sound devoid of mockery. "I suspected as much from the way you chose my watch for parts when I had you fix the navigation tool. No, my dear, you have not lost your knack. There's something here we don't yet understand, but I hope in time we will."

When he tucked the watch away, she let out a moan half filled with relief and half pain.

"I am sorry, Miss Samantha, but I did warn you. I have few enough pocket watches to sacrifice another to your talents, for all I do keep a couple spares. Losses happen even without a Natural having joined the crew."

He rose, towering over Sam in her slumped pose. "I'd planned for more today, but I think it's been trying enough. Why don't you go find Mister Bowden and work at his labors? I suspect it will be less grueling than solving this puzzle no matter how much I wish we could continue."

And with that, Sam knew herself dismissed.

She left drained both of energy and fear compared to when she'd entered the cabin. She had much to think about.

Still, despite all its agonies, she was grateful her talent had not abandoned her here so far from home. She'd lost everything else because of it and could not face losing her knack as well.

34

N at saw Sam appear in the captain's doorway well before dark had fallen. His hands and feet took him down off the ropes without thinking, and he dropped to the deck, a question from Phil echoing in his ears.

"Samantha? Are you okay?"

She looked up at him, her expression distracted, almost confused. She didn't even protest his accidental use of her full name.

Nat caught her arm and pulled Sam over to a coil of rope. "Here. Sit down. What is it? He didn't hurt you, did he?"

If the captain had done something, Nat didn't know what he'd do. He owed his loyalty to Captain Paderwatch from even before Nat had joined the ship. But this was Samantha.

She shook her head as she sank to the rope nest, sending a bolt of pure relief through him, but it didn't change how she looked.

"What happened then?"

The answer came out in slow, quiet phrases as she told him of her failure. Even her reaction to the watch didn't seem to have eased her concerns.

Nat sank to the deck next to her and dropped a hand against her bare foot, the nearest part of her to him. "Let's think this through. When you found the flint, you said you hadn't touched aether since the pump. And a stone isn't the same as metal. Maybe you just needed some time."

Her brow furrowed as she contemplated what he'd said, but ultimately she dismissed it with a wave of her hand. "It wasn't like that. The stones are different, but this just...it didn't have enough aether to sense."

Nat rose with a grin, tugging her to her feet as well. "That's it then. If every bit of metal always had the aether, we'd have always had Naturals, or rather the fear of them. If it were common. Mechanical transformations didn't start until we replaced buckets with pumps and the like." He chose the last to remind her of her recent work, sign enough to his mind her knack stayed as strong as ever.

"I suppose."

He started back toward the rigging and his duties, Sam at his side.

"There would have been more than the occasional clock-maker."

He glanced back at her. "What's that?"

She laced fingers through the twisted ropes, finding a solid hold as he'd taught her. "It's just something Henry said after seeing me work. He thought that's why clock workings draw me so strongly."

"Like how you chose the captain's watch."

"And why he used one to show me I hadn't lost my connection. Henry thinks before the mechanical contraptions grew so complicated, only timepieces had enough strength to gather aether. So the crazy watchmakers were the first Naturals. But their draw was so limited no one realized it was more than just extraordinary skill in a skilled craft."

"I see you've brought another pair of hands."

Nat glanced up at the interruption to find Phil hanging from a new spot, laughing.

"I'm sorry," Nat stammered, realizing he'd left in the middle of stringing a new length of sail rope so they could swap out a bit too frayed to hold should they run into another storm.

Phil grinned wide enough to split his face. "I understood as soon as I saw what drew you off the ropes like a magnet." He flipped upside down so his back stretched against the mast. "Hello, Miss Samantha—Sam, I mean. Come to give this boy a hand?"

She giggled, delighted by his antics as much as if he were an acrobat in one of the traveling shows her father had taken her to. "I've come to try, but I don't know how much use I'll be. I certainly can't do that."

Phil winked, demonstrating better than any words how he'd gained his reputation with the dock women at pretty much every port where they dropped anchor. "I promise to do all the feats. You have only to pass me the length of rope your admirer dropped."

She cast around for it, but Nat, heat burning from his neck to his ears, climbed to where the length dangled from the last guide he'd laced it through.

At least Phil had finished the task Nat set for himself in breaking whatever glum mood had taken Sam over.

35

Nat's talking to, and Phil's antics, went far in distracting Sam from the question of what happened with the pieces. She listened to the stories the riggers swapped over a fish fry and held her own when they asked her for a tale because Jenson had mentioned she knew a few. But through it all, some part of her mind kept churning.

As the evening passed and even long after Nat locked her into her room, Sam turned the question over and over, exploring all angles.

She'd forgotten about the watchmakers until Nat pointed out how Naturals were unknown. And if only watches used to have the complexity necessary to gather aether, maybe it dissipated from a broken object as well.

Sam had noticed a connection between aether and the strong emotions of those around the objects, but what if it was more than that?

Long into the night, until exhaustion forced her eyes closed, she examined the question much like a mechanical object she'd been driven to transform. And the moment she opened her eyes to the sound of the lock turning in her door, her distraction returned.

She scrambled upright, dragging her clothes on by feel so, in the time it took Nat to knock after unlocking the door, she was ready.

"Come in," she called, shoving fingers through her hair so she could tie it back.

Nat held up the lantern, surprised to see her standing. "So eager for the next day?" he teased.

Sam shook her head. "Not for whatever you have planned. I need to talk to the captain."

He frowned at her for a moment as if waiting for more.

"It's about the aether," she said, unable to stand the silence.

Even staying still proved too much as she started to pace. "I've been thinking about why the broken machine had too little aether, and why it lost its voice. Remember how Henry told me about the watchmakers being the first Naturals because clocks had the most complexity? The mechanism the captain has is so broken. It has been apart for too long. Maybe it didn't have enough complexity to gather more than the wisp I first noticed, not enough to develop a single wish, much less a demand for any form at all. I never really thought about it until you pointed it out, but not every bit of metal talks. Not every object demands to be reformed. And even of those that do, some have stronger voices than others."

She pulled out the rock and waved it in his direction. "Sometimes they get more strength from the person who claims them, absorbing emotions and aether that way, but what if it's not so simple? What if they require something more? What if—"

Nat put up a hand for her to stop and laughed.

Before she could take offense, he said, "You're right. You need to talk to the captain. He's the one who wants to figure you out, and apparently you're just as eager for the process. As much as I want to hear what you're thinking, Captain Paderwatch would have my head if I let you spill it out here where he's not present. Come on. I think Jenson just sent up the captain's breakfast, so he should be in his cabin."

Sam felt as if she would explode with all her thoughts and questions. Where a bout made her focus down to the smallest bit and the world dropped away around her, this hit her as a blast of different possibilities, each as distracting as the last and with no way to act on any of it. And without acting, she could not put it in its place or push any of the ideas away.

She raced up the stairs, aware of Nat following at his own pace behind her. Sam wanted to yell at him to hurry up, but then he was carrying the lantern and, lit or not, could not chance the oil.

At the top of the stairs, she paused long enough for him to come up on the deck and set the lantern aside in an alcove made for the purpose. As soon as he had though, Sam looped his arm with hers and tugged him toward the captain's cabin, the door to which stood open to catch the morning breeze.

Nat held her back when they reached the opening, knocking twice.

"Mister Bowden, I can see you standing out there. Come in. And Miss Samantha. I had not thought to have our session in the morning, but since you're here…"

He rose as he spoke, wiping his mouth with a clean handkerchief. "You can be on your way, Mister Bowden."

Nat cleared his throat. "Would you mind if I stayed, sir? Sam told me some of what she's been thinking on this, and I'd appreciate being able to see it through. I might even offer a helping hand, if you'll let me."

Captain Paderwatch raised his eyebrows, but then gestured for both of them to settle down where they could.

Sam stepped forward to take her chair, already scanning the desk to see how he'd pushed all the pieces as close as they could be and placed books around them so no bits could roll away. "I've been thinking on why the mechanism lacked enough aether to talk to me."

The captain quirked a smile. "So you've given up the notion you're somehow damaged and have lost your knack?"

She shrugged. "I suppose so, though it could still be weakened."

"Now, Miss Samantha—Sam. It'll do no good for you to dwell on such things when we both know them to be false. Why, the way you responded to my pocket watch was enough proof to stand up to any scrutiny, even yours."

She flushed a little, but then steamed ahead with her thoughts. "See, the watch set me to considering what has aether and what does not...well, that and something Nat said." Sam told him all about Henry's theory about watchmakers, and her own of people's emotions drawing more aether to the objects around them.

"Hmm. So you think because this machine is not in constant use, and because I have no more than an idle curiosity about its purpose, it cannot collect the material that allows you to interact? Interesting."

"It's more than that," Sam said, reaching out to pick up a gear from the pile. She found no more aether today than had been there the previous day so strict proximity of parts had not improved the situation.

"Explain it to me."

"Well, if only watches were complex enough to draw aether before, and if this mechanism has been not just broken but scattered into pieces..."

"Ah ha," the captain said with enough enthusiasm to make Sam jump. "So it's not complex enough is what you're saying. Just because it once was doesn't mean it will always be. Mister Bowden, you were right. You are needed."

He swept his meal aside without another thought to make space for the pieces and a third person hovering over the desk surface. "Let's make a complicated machine out of it."

36

*U*ntil that moment, Nat had felt much the interloper. Mister Trupt had been expecting him on deck and sitting there listening to the two of them piece together the questions of the universe felt indulgent, the very thing the leaders of industry had attempted to work out of his class.

Sam and Captain Paderwatch looked at him with an expectant air, the demand for his presence no simple act of pity.

A grin stretched his face as he moved into the spot the captain had opened.

Sam had difficulty working without the guidance of aether, and the captain had much more will than ability. This, then, was what he could offer.

"Let's sort the pieces out first," Nat said with as much authority as he could muster. They needn't know he felt his way through this. It would only make their confidence falter. Given enough time, he'd be able to figure out what it had been.

As if reading his thoughts, the captain said, "I'll give you the same grounding I gave Miss Samantha yesterday. I don't remember what this was and have no need for it. We don't have to try to recreate it. Just rebuild it."

"And make it complicated," Sam added, her tone halfway between delight and determination.

Nat accepted the challenge. "Complicated I can do." He looked at the collection of pieces Sam was sorting out and added, "Especially with a collection like this."

He joined in the sorting at first, but then going by instinct, he took one gear from the nearest pile, a rod from another, a spring, and then another gear. Nat wondered if this was how Sam felt when she fell into a bout. If excitement curled in her belly and a deep satisfaction buoyed her up. Sure when she did it, the aether guided her into complexity while he used a guess and a prayer, but in both cases they created something.

They worked in silence, the captain and Sam mimicking his choices as they drew out the same types of pieces and started working them together. Nat pushed aside the idea of a machine and saw instead the pieces of a wooden puzzle like his mother had purchased to help teach him geography.

The passage of time escaped his notice until his stomach gave a loud grumble. They'd come here straight from collecting Sam, and neither of them had eaten anything since the previous night.

The captain sat back and stretched, his bones clicking as they became unbound.

Sam paused as well, or so he thought until Nat realized he held the last two remaining pieces in his hand. It took but a moment to find a connection point for the spring. The gear proved a bit harder if it were to be anything beyond ornamental. Still, when he lifted his hands away, Nat grinned at the impressive structure they'd built.

"It's certainly complicated," Captain Paderwatch said. "I can't even follow the lines of it."

They both turned to face Sam, but her expression stole away Nat's delight.

"What's wrong with it?" He almost didn't want to ask. Whether it could do anything beyond sit there and turn, he couldn't have said, and suspected not, but the form itself remained impressive…to him and the captain.

Sam raised a hand to poke at the mechanism and Nat fought the desire to slap her away.

She didn't make contact. She stroked the shape without once brushing even the pieces that protruded.

Her movements caught hold of him, almost hypnotic in their precision. Always close but not touching until he half wanted to nudge her off balance so she'd stop treating his creation as if it would bite her.

Finally, after an agonizing wait, she sat back on the chair, the epitome of dejection.

"What is it?" he asked again, this time determined to get an answer. "What's wrong with the machine?"

Her shoulders rose only to lower again in a shrug. "It has no spark, no aether. No life at all."

Nat pushed down a smile at her dramatic words. "We just finished building it. Maybe it takes time. You're expecting too much."

She jerked to her feet, reaching back to steady the chair as if it would crash into the captain's map case despite the bolts holding it fast to the floor. "I am not. We've been working on this for hours, Nat. And you'd have to be blind not to see it's complicated. If it were going to collect aether, our shared intensity should have offered a feast of the stuff."

"Miss Samantha, we are unsure of the method this aether uses. Could it be as Mister Bowden claims? Could it just require a longer stretch of time, maybe without us hovering over it?"

"He's wrong."

Her conviction thrust a dagger at the heart of Nat's pride. He swallowed hard before saying what needed to be said.

"Perhaps it's my fault. Perhaps this isn't the sort of complicated it needed, or perhaps I don't have what it takes to awaken the aether."

Sam looked at him with sorrow in her eyes, and he wondered if she pitied him until she spoke.

"You forget, Nat." She pushed a hand into one of her pockets as if fighting the urge to punch him as she had when he teased her about looking like a wild child. Or so he thought until she pulled free the piece of flint he'd given her. "You managed to draw aether into a stone. A dead stone even. If you're not the problem here, I must be."

She raised her arm as if to throw the flint at the desk, and Nat pushed his hand under hers, afraid the stone wouldn't survive the impact. At the last moment, she lowered it gently to the surface just beyond his palm.

Like Sam, the flint rested so close and yet not touching his creation, not breaking the invisible cloak she'd drawn around it. This stone didn't want to brush against what he'd created any more than Sam had. Not that a stone would have any way to react, but still, he felt the burn.

"Do I need to sacrifice another watch before you give up this fool idea, Miss Samantha? If a Natural could run out of the knack, there'd be withered men, women, and children stumbling out of the asylums in a desperate attempt to claim a normal life. Have you ever heard of a Natural recovering? I can't say I have, and I've spent a few more years on this earth than you have."

Nat had looked to the captain when he started speaking, but turned then to encourage Sam to listen.

Only Sam was not listening.

She was as far from listening as possible, her thoughts having turned inward much like when she'd been in a bout except for the lack of joy in her expression.

"I've never heard of a Natural who could transform stone either," the captain said, his mind moving to the next puzzle despite his threat.

When Captain Paderwatch reached around the machine to pick up Sam's gift, Nat wanted to snatch it away. But he could think of no explanation for his behavior the other man would accept.

The awkward angle meant the captain's fingers brushed the stone without claiming it.

Finally, something broke the barrier and touched his machine.

Nat stifled an unexpected surge of joy, unaware of the extent this had bothered him until the moment was over. Such was his reaction, though, he failed to notice how the captain had jerked back until he saw the stone still there.

Captain Paderwatch shook his hand, mumbling something about a charge, but movement in the corner of his eye pulled Nat's attention back to Sam.

Where before she looked as if she faced the noose, now her eyes sparkled with energy as she stared at the machine they'd built.

37

Sam had been so sure she'd understood what made aether collect around an object. She'd thought she'd figured it all out. But when the complicated machine hadn't gathered anything, even with Nat's help, she'd given up.

And then everything had changed.

The aether collected at the base of Nat's machine tasted of
him. She knew the energy, had lived with it tucked in her
pocket, her touchstone. Whenever things seemed at their
worst, she'd drawn on his strength, the strength he'd given her.

Her fingers reached for the stone once again, but she
pulled them back.

The construction needed the stored aether more than she
did. Just as the stone came back to life after being ripped from
its bed, it now brought the machine they'd put together to life,
or life of a sort.

"Is it working?"

The question barely scraped her mind for a moment, comprehension coming as an echo of the words.

She couldn't find strength in her touchstone, but she had
another source in Nat.

Sam reached for his hand and he met her halfway, accepting the touch without comment.

As he'd done before, Nat grounded her, better even than
Lily ever had. Her jumble of thoughts found patterns and her
tongue figured out how to form a single word.

"Yes."

The sound came out harsh and rough.

Sam concentrated, swallowing hard before she tried again. "Yes. It's working. The stone…somehow it's acting as a siphon, taking scattered aether and feeding it to the machine."

"Yes!"

Sam lost her grip as Nat surged to his feet, acting as if the failure had been his rather than hers. She paused in the thought, realizing neither had been to blame. The stone gathered aether so quickly because of its nature, and that same nature allowed it to feed the newly created machine. The stone had its own knack.

Nat turned his focus back on her, catching hold of both of Sam's hands. "So what does it want to be?"

She shook her head back and forth slowly, the question one she'd already started to wonder.

What they'd built she doubted even Nat knew. The gears might turn if they hadn't bound any against another, but what function or purpose it might serve lay outside of her understanding. But the aether was too fresh, too new, to communicate even something as simple as the knowledge of what it collected.

"It doesn't know, does it?" Nat asked when she'd clearly held silent for too long. "Not even aether can make sense of what I designed."

He sounded so glum she couldn't help the laugh that escaped, drawing her fully out of the aether's grip, an event only possible because of the immature state.

"You were right after all. It needs time to gather the aether, and time to form ideas once it lays claim to enough. The stone is different somehow. It holds the aether but doesn't use it. And then it gives what it's gathered up and collects more."

"Fascinating."

The exhalation from the captain startled Sam. She'd forgotten his presence, aware only of Nat and the aether growing in front of her.

"What I mean to say is," she tried again, "it may find its purpose once it gets used to the aether, claims it rather than just accepting what the stone passes on."

"So the stone is broken again."

Sam laughed in the face of Nat's despair before she got herself under control. "No. The stone is no more broken than it was when you plucked it from the rock, less so because I think it still holds some of what you gave it. It could be the echo from your structure though. I don't think the stone can be broken. Used up for a bit, maybe, but not broken."

Nat frowned at her. "What happened then when we removed it? You said we'd killed the stone."

She brushed her fingers across the back of his hand. "I was wrong. Maybe you hadn't taken it from the aether at all. Maybe I drew out its aether when lying there. I wouldn't have known how to use it because I had no vessel to put it in, so the aether could have just evaporated."

As though he finally understood what she was saying, Nat stared at the machine he'd begun and they'd all three had a hand in. "So it's working, then?"

Sam lifted her shoulders in another shrug. "It doesn't have a voice yet, but it has aether. All I know, all I've learned my whole life, tells me aether comes first and the voice second. The mechanisms are no more able to speak than a baby can."

That brought back the memory of why she had thought her sister was casting her aside only to learn rather than being pregnant, Lily felt herself too ill to protect Sam any longer. Nat might have recovered from his glum mood, but it seemed to be sinking into her. Why couldn't she have figured all this out before leaving her sister? Then she might have had the control to stay and help.

"Well, then," the captain said. "This has been a fascinating morning, but from the angle of the sun, it's almost midday. My porridge is cold and thick, and yours never even made it to the bowl. Why don't the two of you go off and give Jenson a hand. Maybe he'll have some bread for you to snack on in the meantime."

Grateful for the distraction, Sam headed for the door, pausing at the last moment to check if Nat followed after.

"And Miss Samantha, let's give this structure a day to gather its wits about it. I'm sure Mister Trupt can find enough to keep the two of you busy, especially with me having claimed you since daybreak."

38

The afternoon dragged on for Nat even after he'd had his fill of bread and stew. Tasks that used to spark his imagination now seemed nothing less than drudge work when he knew he'd created something complicated enough to draw aether. Maybe Sam no longer felt the pull when she'd done this sort of thing a thousand times or more, but he'd never put together something strong enough, or if he had, he'd been ignorant of its true nature.

The captain had declared they'd wait a full day.

Nat didn't know if he could last so long.

They scrubbed the deck, penance for not warning Mister Trupt of their absence in the morning. They patched sails, coiled ropes, even fished off the bow, but through it all, Nat's attention was on the captain's door. What he expected to happen, he did not know, but he couldn't turn away, arranging his position with the cabin always in his sights.

Then, just before Jenson brought the evening meal up on the deck, Captain Paderwatch left his cabin with a purposeful stride in Nat's direction.

Nat leapt to his feet, spilling the fishing net he'd been mending into a tangle of strands and earning a curse from Sven who'd been working at their side.

"Sam, he comes for us."

He surprised a stunned look on her face, but what else could it be?

The captain strode right by them with hardly a nod to recognize their presence. Off he went to speak with Mister Trupt about who knew what, leaving Nat standing struck dumb.

"He said tomorrow."

Her quiet statement offered little comfort as Nat settled back into the work as antsy as he'd ever been and lacking in focus. He paid attention soon enough though when he thrust the mending needle through the skin of his finger instead of where he'd meant to send it.

Cursing, he sucked on the wound and promised silently to do better, if only so he wouldn't be too injured to work with the machine come morning.

For all she laughed at Nat for his eagerness, Sam met the morning with the same sense of anticipation. She'd never watched the path of a mechanical object before, remaining oblivious until the moment when it caught her attention and demanded her service. She found herself in new territory along with the captain and Nat. She wanted to understand as much as they did if not more.

The captain swung his door wide the moment they knocked, making it seem as if he'd been waiting on the other side, and maybe he had been.

"Come in, come in. I had Jenson send three servings here today so none of us will starve or be weakened by hunger." His face split into a grin, proving age no restraint on anticipation.

When he moved out of the way, though, disappointment struck deep. Nat's construction was no longer in its place on the desk.

Her feelings must have been stark on her face because the captain glanced her way and laughed, shaking his head at the same time.

"I thought it best we eat without the distraction. I neither want porridge all over my desk nor a mechanical tool I have to fight the sea birds for because of the grains wound into its very structure."

As much as Sam wanted to protest, his logic seemed sound. Still, acceptance didn't stop her from wolfing down her portion, nor Nat from doing the same. This decision proved faulty when the two of them had to sit quietly while the captain made methodical progress through his own serving as though unaware of his audience.

Always the gentleman, Captain Paderwatch dabbed his face clean with a handkerchief.

His action made Sam aware of her own appearance. She licked her lips to remove any excess and rubbed her face on a sleeve only to meet the captain's raised eyebrows when she lowered her arm.

"If I didn't know better, Miss Samantha, I'd be thoroughly taken in by your charade."

She let him think her actions a result of her attempt to appear the boy. He didn't need to know Lily had been trying to scold it out of her since she left the rough environment of a barn where she'd spent many months as a child. She'd hid there from those who would have caged her for the very reason this man courted her presence.

"Well, then, shall we get to it?"

The captain didn't need an answer and might have appreciated silence better than the eager shouts from both Nat and Sam, but he said nothing as he twisted to raise the lid on a trunk set beside his desk.

"I took the liberty of adding in two of my less valuable machines," he said as he lowered the unfamiliar contraptions to the desk surface before reaching for another. "Just in case enough time has not yet passed."

Sam barely heard the rest of his statement, her gaze fixed on the two then three mechanical constructs before her. Her head ached with the force of their clamors, no question remaining about her ability to hear the aether-driven demands.

The first served some purpose as a chart reader as far as she could tell from the images it sent into her mind. It was old, older than any mechanism she'd ever touched. Many hands had held it, many prayers imbuing the metal's aether with imprints. It had the strongest voice, but a blend of so many hopes it dissolved into cacophony.

The second had fewer imprints. She could detect only one for sure, that of Captain Paderwatch, though she sensed at least one more as a shadow presence. She could not understand what its purpose had been, but what it wanted to become, and how she could make the wish come to be, came through as clear as the water around the island.

When she turned her focus on Nat's construction, Sam gasped at the sharp images it had grown to send, each one bearing Nat's imprint as if she and the captain had had no hand in the making.

Sam laughed aloud at what it wanted to be, surprised, delighted, and confident all at once. This one would become something wonderful.

Nat touched her hand, pulling Sam from the aether daze long enough to make out his expression.

"What is it?" he asked. "Does it live?"

"Yes. It lives. They all three are swelling with purpose. Can I? Do I have your permission to give them what they desire?"

She looked to the captain at the last, though the one she wanted to devote her attention to belonged more to Nat than any other no matter who had owned the original machine making up its pieces.

"Absolutely. I ask only you speak of what it is like while you work so we can learn from it."

Fighting the pull of the objects, Sam said, "I will do my best," before she lost the ability to ignore their cries.

The world slipped away, or rather it narrowed to the three objects and their competing demands on her time.

She'd never faced three at once, and certainly not ones she could act on. She'd never had to choose which demand to follow even when she fought the demand in favor of the repairs requested of her since being discovered. For a moment, it thrust her back into the bilge room with machines lining the wall, whispering, crying out, and demanding all at once but none within reach. She pushed away the memory to focus on what lay before her.

Her heart wanted to dive into Nat's construct, but at the last moment she realized she'd be trapped in the draw of the other two, the permission given her stripping away the last of her resistance. If she wanted to be present in mind as well as body when he saw what his desires had shed onto the machine, she had to tame the other two first.

Sam began with the younger of the two, and the one with the clearest vision between them. Aether offered a path, guiding her to the correct part and aiding her in the changes, all of which she tried to speak. Whether her words made any sense or were even audible, she didn't know.

A deep sense of relief filled her as the answers appeared and the pieces came together one after another until she'd achieved the request of this machine, success apparent by how the demand transformed into satisfaction, the closest to happiness she'd felt from any of her creations.

What it had become remained unknown to her, but Sam had done her part. The captain would have to figure out the result.

She didn't rest. She couldn't with the other two calling to her.

Time passed, whether fast or slow, she didn't know, only half aware of the stream of words coming from her mouth and the faint scritch of nib against parchment. What claimed her full attention was the second machine, the one whose request had been muddled, buried under the clear demand from the first.

As she'd hoped, without a clutter of aether-driven demands, the mix of voices calling from the second machine settled into a single desire. Part of her wondered if the imprints had negotiated among themselves to make the choice, though what Nat and the captain would make of such a question as she said it, she could not imagine.

An image formed clear enough for her to understand this object wanted to better accomplish its tasks, having held the role of assisting in the interpretation of charts far too long to abandon the post. Transformation would have been easier than the minute adjustments she had to make, but soon this too had accepted its new state.

4o

Nat thought he'd be bored and fidgeting, but the captain had them both transcribing everything Sam said. She spoke so quickly, he was hard-pressed to get even the gist of it down. The distraction of what she was doing didn't help either.

Her hands moved so quickly they seemed blurred in the rapidly dimming cabin, and the transformations in the machines before her occurred like magic. He could neither see what she did nor understand the purpose of her changes, but that she changed, and that the machines seemed somehow better, stronger, and more powerful could not be denied.

When he could no longer see the page in front of him, Nat went by instinct, hoping his scratches would make some kind of sense when reviewed later. The captain neither stopped to light a lantern nor suggested Nat did.

Then she pulled forward the mechanism he'd come to think of as his for all the three of them worked equally in creating it. No matter how much he tried to turn his attention back to the writing, neither his gaze nor his thoughts complied.

His pen kept writing. What he recorded, he had no idea.

If anything, her hands moved faster, her lips curving into a grin as she undid all their hard work.

Nat didn't even think to protest. He'd seen what she'd done with the others. Whatever she did now would only make the mechanism better even if her intensity made him uncomfortable.

The pieces came together one by one into a form that tweaked something in the back of his mind, a form his memory recognized even before his mind did.

But when he saw it fully, a startled laugh burst from him much as it had from Sam earlier.

She laid the foundation for a ship.

Layer by layer, gears and struts where cargo and storage would have been, Sam built not just any ship, but the very one they sailed upon.

The silence beyond her frantic murmur brought Nat back to awareness from his admiration of the paddle wheels added to each side before they vanished into the casings. He glanced over to find the captain just as enraptured and Sam's words flowing unheard.

Nat squinted down at the paper and started writing once again, trying to capture as much as he could remember.

His efforts were soon joined by the scritch of the captain's pen, and the three of them were once more lost in the amazing process of creation occurring before their eager eyes.

Soon the upper deck came to be, and finally sails, though these hung loose for lack of a wind to stretch the cloth.

She let out a long sigh as if she'd been holding her breath the whole time and slumped against the table.

Nat lowered his pen, becoming aware of a fierce cramp in his hand, but the exhilaration of being in the same space as the beautiful structure before him washed away any exhaustion.

He glanced around at the pages scattered throughout the room for the ink to dry without smearing, having no memory of spreading his share.

Captain Paderwatch reached for the sand box to dust the last pages, but his fingers scraped the desk. He cursed then laughed as Nat turned to see what had caused his reaction.

The deck planks, made of wood and perfectly formed, had to have come from somewhere. She'd been surprised to learn she could affect stone. Wood had a very different nature from what she'd said, but he'd seen her draw on nearby objects when she needed to. The box containing the captain's sand, fully sealed to protect against water and being thrown about, offered just what she'd needed while the metal clasps holding it together must have given way before her talents.

The captain leaned forward to finger the sails even as Nat turned to examine the fabric as well.

A small stain showed where the captain had wiped a porridge spill from the corner of his mouth, his handkerchief now transformed as much as the mechanism had been.

"She's not to blame," Nat protested before the captain could accuse Sam. "You told her to."

Captain Paderwatch shook his head, but a smile showed he didn't mean to chastise. "She did no more than what I asked of her. It does seem I need to be more careful of what I have on hand before opening that particular gate."

Though he laughed, Nat remembered the fear in Sam's eyes when she'd awoken from a bout to discover she'd dismantled the captain's watch for parts. He swore silently he'd be more careful too. He'd make sure the only things in reach when she entered the fugue state of a Natural were ones available for her use.

They both turned to look at her, waiting for some contribution, but she lay with her head on the table, if not asleep, then too exhausted to say a word.

"Mister Bowden, it seems to me our Natural needs some nourishment to replace what she must have burned through. From the lack of sunlight, I'd guess it's right around supper. Would you be so kind as to check with Jenson regarding victuals?"

Nat leapt to his feet and reached the door faster than he would have thought possible, but he hesitated before going through. "Can I show it to the men? The ship I mean?"

He didn't know whether he asked the captain or Sam, but the same answer came from both sets of lips.

"It's yours."

The captain continued, "The mechanism is yours, Nat. You had the original making of it, and from what Miss Samantha said during her work, its vision came through you." He barked a single laugh. "And to think your mother thought you'd be better suited to the railroads."

Nat's cheeks ached with the force of his grin as he swept up the ship and burst through the door on the way to Jenson. She'd wanted him to work on trains for little reason beyond that he'd be closer to home. The sea had always been his dream, and now he had proof the ship claimed him down to his very soul.

41

As luck would have it, when Nat opened the door, Sam could see sailors gathering on deck for the meal. She pushed to her feet, hands shaking and knees weak.

"Miss Samantha, I can have a serving brought to us here. No need to stir."

Despite the captain's words, Nat had already stepped through the door, his prize clutched in both hands.

Sam wanted to see the crew's reaction. She had yet to gain confidence in their decision to keep her. The captain and Nat she felt sure of, but one mistake and the others might see her work as a danger even when they'd considered her a gem only moments before.

"Jenson," she heard Nat call out. "Set aside a plate of stew for Samantha, would you? Just look at what she made me."

She chuckled under her breath at his continued use of her full name. Had they been cast off together, her ruse at being a boy would have lasted less than a heartbeat.

Captain Paderwatch gave a laugh of his own, making her aware of how she'd crossed to the door to follow. "I suppose the two of you have spent enough time penned up in here. Go on. Better get your stew before Nat has Jenson tied up with admiring the model and the pot goes unattended."

"I can serve my own portion."

"I'm sure you can seeing as you've been a help to the cook often enough, but it would make him sour to think he'd failed in his duties. Run along quickly, now. And pass word I'm ready for my own, would you? I fear Mister Bowden may have neglected to communicate the need."

Sam nodded her agreement, touched her forehead as she'd seen the others do for respect, and ducked through the door.

The sight that greeted her could be nothing less than gratifying.

Full bowls were ignored, either clutched in hands or abandoned where they'd been sitting, the sailors having leapt up to see what Nat showed off. A quick scan of faces showed no fear she could see.

The engineer remained perched in his lonely vigil at the bow, but she hadn't expected him to join in with anything concerning her.

"Sam," Jenson called out to her. "Come get your portion. I want a better look at this thing that has the men ignoring my efforts."

She half expected a scowl on his face, but instead the cook gave her a wink.

Sam smiled back. "The captain requests his portion as well."

Then came the scowl, though only for a heartbeat before the cook closed his thick fingers over the shoulder of one of the younger sailors. "Get this to the captain. Be quick about it," he growled, shoving the bowl he'd prepared for Sam into the man's unsuspecting hands.

"And now for you, Sam, then I'm done. You're the last few anyways, and Mister Bowden's too busy to worry about his meal any time soon."

"Thank you." Sam took the bowl and chose an out-of-the-way spot where she could watch the others.

The rich scent, with a hint of spices gathered from the island, made her aware of just how empty her stomach lay. The exclamations could not hold her interest compared to the sustenance before her. Sam swallowed down the large portion in rapid scoops, remembering too late how Nat had warned her against scarfing food.

Her stomach roiled once, but she'd burned enough energy in the workings it chose not to fully rebel. Still, she let the portion settle as much as her gaze brushed over the unattended pot and the chance for a second serving.

A low whistle drew her back to the crowd around Nat only to find they'd taken a step back.

Her stomach twinged once more, wondering what her contraption had done to make them fear it.

"Do that again, Mister Bowden. Do it now when all can see."

The demand first came from Phil, but many others echoed it or nodded their approval.

The tension inside Sam uncoiled, and she leaned forward for a better view. Though she'd created the model, her actions were driven by aether, and even she didn't know the whole of it.

Nat lifted the ship up high enough to make it visible even from where Sam stood. He shifted something on the side, and she heard the faint scritch of metal parts moving from within, her senses still heightened by the lingering aether.

At first, she couldn't tell what he'd done, and any explanation was lost in the resounding cheers, but he tipped the model to one side and spun in a slow circle, letting her see clearly.

She didn't know what she was looking for until the bottom turned her direction. A laugh burst from her at the sight of the paddles moving of their own accord. She doubted it had the water-tight nature necessary to float, but the model worked much like the real ship.

A vision of her mechanicals, abandoned at Henry's estate, crafting metal boats to sail the seas in hopes of finding Sam crossed her mind, but she shook it off. Even if it were possible, such an event would destroy any good will she'd gained among the crew. This had become her life, and she had more friends now than ever before. She didn't need to build ones out of metal as much as she mourned those she'd left behind.

With that thought, she gave in to her stomach and collected another serving, the captain having passed word she could eat her fill this night.

THE SCRAPE OF A FOOT against the wooden deck gave her scant warning before one of the sailors dropped to sit at her side.

Though he carried a bowl like her own, Sven made no attempt to lift his spoon. Instead, he nodded toward Nat and the crowd. "Could you make one of those for me?"

Whatever she'd expected, the question left Sam without words. The captain had her crafting to study her, much like he'd studied the bugs and plants on the island. All other requests had been as a last resort.

"I wouldn't bother you," he continued after the silence grew oppressive, "but see, I have a boy back in Dover. I don't get to see him often what with the captain taking us to faraway ports. I'd like my son to have something of my life, something to make him think of me fondly."

Her mind flashed back to before she'd stowed away and a young boy on the docks. She'd fixed his train and let it find its person only to have the boy's father reject the toy and set a mob against her.

"I'm not a toymaker." Her voice came out flat, filled more with desperate memories now than the crew's enjoyment.

"Right."

The spoon dove into his stew and milled around there without Sven lifting the bite. Sam glanced at his face and found him crestfallen.

The chatter still surrounding Nat measured harsh against his disappointment, and guilt bit into Sam at how she'd made this sailor pay for a stranger's rejection.

She caught his arm. "I'm not a toymaker." Though she said the same words, her voice softened.

Sven glanced to her, his eyes widening in a hope she needed to see.

"It doesn't have to be anything fancy. I'm a sailor. My son's a sailor's boy. Just something to connect us while I'm away."

Sam gave him a smile as she tried to figure out how to explain. Her words to the captain came back to her, and she shrugged.

"I don't drive the form it takes." She waved at Nat's ship. "It was Nat's will that shaped his mechanical. I give them what they need to be."

His lips firmed, and Sven nodded once. "You don't have to explain. It's not for the likes of me. I understand."

She jumped to her feet, surprising both of them.

"That's not what I said, and not what I meant," Sam scolded, borrowing Lily's tone to do so. "I can't promise anything because it's the device that calls out for a shape. But I never said I wouldn't try."

A deep red crept up beneath the sailor's tan.

"Sorry," he mumbled, looking like a chastened stable boy.

Sam knelt at his side and caught one of his hands. "If you have something built of metal, something you carry with you, perhaps it will find a form your son could enjoy. And more than that, it would carry something of you within it. It's how my knack works. Your wishing, dreams, and desires take form in the mechanical."

Her words clearly made him uncomfortable, and he shifted away at first, but just when she'd despaired of fixing the situation, he froze.

"I have just the thing. It's not large and has maybe too few pieces, but I got it for him already. Only when it came time to give it over, I couldn't. It's nothing he would treasure. Just a wind-up I found in an African port. I didn't want him to think less of me for it. Would that do?"

Sam held back a cry of joy at what she'd seen as a rejection turning into an answer. She remembered how the first device the captain brought forth had no aether, though, and caution made her wise.

"I'll have to see it first to figure out if I can make anything from it." Then she remembered Nat's efforts which gave his mechanical dreams. "If not, perhaps Mister Bowden could craft something from the pieces your son might find more appealing."

Sven scrambled to his feet, the now cold stew still clutched in one hand. "I'll go fetch it," he said. "You wait right here. I'll be back."

She watched him rush off, overlaying his eagerness and that of the other sailors with the horrible day on the docks. People shoved her about when they didn't know and chasing after her once they did.

She hadn't chosen this ship out of all the others. Her feet found the gangplank and raced up it with no thought in her head. But she couldn't have found a better place, a better people.

They'd overcome their fears to accept her, and she'd do everything in her power to live up to their trust.

"You're making Sven a device?"

The question startled Sam out of her thoughts, and she glanced up to see one of the other sailors.

"He asked me to make something for his son. I said I would try."

"Would you make something for me girl? She gets so lonely when I'm out to sea."

"I wouldn't mind a model of my own," Mister Trupt added as he came to join the sailors now gathering around Sam.

She flashed a grin round at them. "I'd be happy to try. I just need something made of metal you've spent some time with, but I can't promise what form it'll take."

"Be careful what you offer these fools," Phil said from her side. "They'll keep you so busy you'll have no time for the captain, and he's the final word in everything on the ship."

Sven returned then, his large hands clutched around something much smaller than what she'd had for Nat's.

"She agreed to do mine first," he said within moments of taking in the crowd.

"And so she will." Mister Trupt's voice quieted all others. "But she's worked hard for the captain all day, and from how clean her bowl's been scraped, I'd guess she's tired and hungry. There will be no more doing her knack today, and this will not interfere with her work for the captain or any other chores."

He gave her a stern look, spoiling the weight with a quick wink. "Now get to your suppers, and no complaining if they're cold. Tomorrow's another full day."

The sailors melted into the darkness to recover their various bowls while Mister Trupt caught Sam's arm and swept up her bowl as he tugged her toward the pot. "You can't let them take advantage of you, Miss Samantha. They are like sharks with opportunity being blood in the water. As it is, I'll have to make limits on the number of devices brought on from each port or people will talk. It's more important than ever before that no gossip comes our way with you as a permanent member of the crew."

Warmth spread through Sam's body at his words, meaning more from him than any other. The captain might have the final say, but the first mate ran the ship. His word meant law.

"Get yourself another bowl then off to your hammock. I won't have any complaints tomorrow, you hear me?"

Sam nodded her agreement as Mister Trupt strode off, leaving her to serve up a third bowlful. Her efforts were interrupted, though, when she realized Nat was involved in doing the same.

"He gave me a talking to as well for keeping the sailors from their food. Don't take it too harshly."

Sam flashed Nat a smile as she took the ladle from his hand. He hadn't been paying attention to the rest, or he wouldn't have worried. Mister Trupt, and the whole of the crew, accepted her as no one ever had before, not even her sister and Henry.

The first mate would hear no complaints from her now or ever. And she needn't worry about her knack building to the point of danger with sailors lined up to give her something to change. She'd left Henry's estate in search of a safe haven, and though it lay not on the Continent nor even on solid ground, she'd found one after all.

Thank You for Reading

Thank you for reading *Gifts*. I hope you enjoyed how the first major story arc came together, but have no fear. There is more coming for Sam and Nat soon enough.

I love to hear about your experiences with my characters, so drop me a line in email to:

  * author@margaretmcgaffeyfisk.com

or use the contact form on:

  * margaretmcgaffeyfisk.com

And while you are there, if you sign up for my monthly newsletter, I'll share a bit of my writing and publishing journey, fun events, and even snippets or pre-publication stories as a thank you for letting me into your inbox. You can also choose to receive release announcements, which are split into genre and go out only when a new title is available in that genre. Feel free to select as many options as you'd like.

Finally, can I ask a favor? If you're willing, I'd appreciate an honest review of *Gifts*. Your feedback will help The Steamship Chronicles find the right audience. If you choose to review on your website as well as retail and/or reader sites, you can also send me the link with permission to include it on that book's information page, if you're so inclined.

If you'd like to read an excerpt from *Life and Law*, Book 4 of The Steamship Chronicles, please turn the page.

Excerpt

Life and Law

Book Four of The Steamship Chronicles

*Sam may have found her place, bringing the first set of The Steamship
Chronicles stories to an end, but what of her sister and Henry left in
England to worry? They have their own stories to tell.*

Henry sat beside Lily on the sitting room sofa, her
head pillowed against his shoulder and her feet
tucked up the same way she'd scolded Sam for many a time.
He stroked her soft blond hair as he spun out yet another tale
of where Sam would be at this very moment, though Lily no
longer heard, having fallen into a doze.

"It's been two days so she should have reached the village
by now. Stuart would have sent my letter ahead. A representa-
tive from the safe haven will be waiting for them, waiting to
bring her to a place where she will finally find freedom." He
told Lily nothing he hadn't said before, and she didn't listen
anyway, but Henry found as much comfort as his wife did in
the knowledge Samantha had found happiness at last.

He missed her more than he would have thought possible,

his parents' estate a solemn place without Sam's laughter and cheeky mischief to brighten it. The servants felt much the same, going about with mournful expressions as though someone had died.

All except Kate.

If that young woman hadn't proved a help and comfort to Lily from the moment they arrived so many years before, he'd have sent her packing back to her father's house in the village just to rid himself of the sight of her smile.

As though fate laughed at him, a quick knock at the open door revealed the lady's maid just then.

Henry shook his head, tipping it toward his sleeping wife, but he couldn't hold back a curse when Kate stepped to one side to reveal none other than Stuart, his man from Dover who should have been with Sam.

Lily stirred against his shoulder, her head lifting free a moment later as she blinked awake. "Henry?"

This time he kept the curse behind his lips but felt it no less.

Freed, Henry pushed to his feet, determined to take Stuart to the study where they could have a private conversation. Clearly his man had not accompanied Sam as they'd planned. For him to have come all this way could only mean bad news. Lily didn't need to hear it in a raw form.

"There's business to discuss. I'll be back in a little while. Kate is here to look after you."

Lily's gaze followed his to the doorway and tension swept her body, clearly recognizing the man's dockside appearance though she'd never met him.

"If it's about my sister, I want to hear it."

For all her frailty, there was no weakness in her tone. Lily had always been far too sharp for him to brush her concerns aside.

Shoulders slumping, Henry waved the man to one of the chairs. "Tell us then."

Stuart moved awkwardly across the room and held his hat on his knees, both hands clutching the short brim.

"I did everything you asked," he said, the words strained, "But the girl didn't come, nor you neither."

The burly man had never seemed so cowed in all the times Henry had met with him.

"I checked where you usually lodge, and no one had seen you. I'd have been here sooner, but I stayed to investigate." He stumbled on the last word, strength and loyalty his qualifications rather than education.

"What did you find?" Henry could tell the man had more to say, but the delay offered no kindness as Lily's breath started to catch in her throat, signs another coughing fit threatened.

Stuart hung his head and stared at his hands for a long moment. "The news ain't good. You would have sent word if you didn't send the girl what with paying for the tickets already and all, so I went out to learn what might have become of her."

"And?"

Finally Stuart looked up to meet his gaze. "I found no word of a girl, but there were a steam carriage crashed something horrible when heading for the docks. From the luggage, I'd say a lady of means were in it, but there weren't nobody by the time I learned of the accident. The police took off the driver and the carriage stood empty. Asked the fellow watching it, and he said no deaths. Nobody found there but the driver. I didn't get a chance to talk to the driver myself, but from all reports, he took a bruising. Wasn't all that clear, if you know what I mean, when they wanted to know the happenings."

Henry exchanged a tortured look with Lily before turning back to Stuart, whose mangled hat would need some pressing before it would recover its former state.

"You are not to blame, Stuart. You did well bringing us this news, and for seeking what had come about." Henry forced his lips into a pained smile. "You must have rushed all the way here. A bed will be found in the servant quarters, and Kate here will take you down to the kitchen for some food."

Kate drew in a sharp breath, but said nothing when Henry leveled his gaze on her. Instead, the lady's maid jerked her chin and set off, expecting Stuart to follow.

Stuart rose, bobbed a rough bow, and half-jogged after the disappearing maid.

Henry released a slow breath, trying to take in all they'd learned as little as it had been.

Stuart had been responsible for negotiating Henry's shipping interests for years. Not the full arrangements or trading plans, but making sure when one of Henry's interests came in the workers were ready to unload and supplies for the necessary restock were available.

The man was thorough and efficient.

Henry never had a moment's doubt when asking him to accompany Sam to the Continent, nor had Stuart questioned the propriety of such arrangements as some would have. He accepted Henry would tell him all he needed to know, nothing more and nothing less.

It had been arranged with sealed letters and reassurances. Stuart remained ignorant as to Sam's true nature. There'd been no reason to stretch his loyalty with such knowledge. Henry knew his staff here would keep silent about Sam as well, their loyalty without question even in the case of Kate.

Still, Stuart's ignorance meant he could not have known to ask the right questions, and the lack of information ate at Henry. Just where could Sam have gone? She'd never been to Dover before, had no one she could turn to beyond Stuart whom she had never met, and he'd seen the flash of fear in her eyes when Lily could not come with her.

A soft groan escaped his lips at the thought of Sam wandering the docks in a town that, while not wealthy, would have its own supply of contraptions if for no other reason than sailors bringing home curiosities from distant lands. With the purse he'd given her as well, Sam could attract the wrong attention all too easily without Stuart to guide her.

*I*CE SURROUNDED LILY, TRAPPING HER frozen in the realization that all their plans had fallen apart. She had no one to blame but herself.

"How can Samantha ever be safe now?"

Lily hadn't meant to say the words out loud, but was too caught up in her own fears to keep them bottled inside her.

Henry let free a quiet groan.

She could feel the tension coiling within him as her head once again found his shoulder.

He kept his touch gentle, wrapping his arms around Lily

and gathering her to him as if he could protect her from this truth the way he'd protected them both from the law all those years before. Only now he could do nothing.

"Sam's a smart girl." Henry's voice rumbled against her ear. "She's able to manage on her own. It hasn't been so many years since she kept quiet in the stables."

As much as she wanted to cling to his reassurance and his warmth, Lily pushed free.

"You don't understand. She was safe in the stables, and though she had little enough to amuse her, she kept calm. Now, she'll be tired and frightened. Maybe even injured in the crash. She won't have me to prevent a bout, and she'll know I won't be coming any time soon either."

Lily swallowed hard, aware of how her voice had risen.

"You've never seen her scared before. Any control she's managed strips away faster than you can blink. How could I have let her go alone?"

Henry caught her hands, holding them tightly even when she tried to tug them free. She had no choice but to meet his earnest gaze and let him see the tears gathering in her eyes.

He smiled, though where he found the strength, she could not fathom. "I know you're worried. I am as well. But look at the truth before us. Listen to what Stuart uncovered."

Lily shook her head, not in denial but rather because confusion swept her. "I do not understand your meaning. He uncovered nothing," she said, her words as faint as her strength had become with this discovery.

Henry released her then only to rise and pace about the room. His arms waved in a sharp punctuation of his words. "When he made inquiries, rumors of the carriage accident had spread through the docks. He learned of it even when he hadn't been present to see the event himself."

She murmured an encouraging sound, clinging to his sense of hope when she had none of her own.

"Don't you see? If Sam had lost control then, the carriage would be the least of the news people would eagerly share. Stuart spoke with a policeman on site. The officer would have at least given warning if news that an out-of-control Natural had been making the rounds. Such a rumor would spread just as quickly as the carriage tale if not more so."

She could see the truth in his statement at last, but still, Lily's tension didn't ease.

Her sister was out there among strangers in a place she knew not at all surrounded by those who would seek to gain from her more than assist her. At least until they learned the truth of her nature. Then they'd be all too ready to assist her into an asylum.

Henry knelt before Lily, catching her hands a second time. "She must be fine. She survived the crash, and if I know my Sam, she figured out some way to get to the Continent with or without my help. Surely she could devise a plan to make inquiries of her own as to her ship. Perhaps Stuart had left his post by the time she found the right vessel, but she's wily enough to sneak aboard on her own. Just think of the trouble she's gotten up to here at the estate. She's no quiet lady no matter how much you'd like to see her so."

"What if she couldn't find it? What if the ship had already sailed when she learned its berth? What if she's wandering the streets of Dover, or already been taken by some ruffian."

Though his shake held little force, Lily's teeth cracked together when she'd thought them already clenched as tight as teeth could be. It did succeed in breaking her of a growing panic as she settled dazed vision on his determined expression.

"Remember how delighted she was with the idea of going, Lily? She wouldn't let something simple like missing her ship stand in her way. She's been dreaming about this as far back as she can remember. Sam used to tell me of it when we first came here. I took her tapering off as a sign she'd found happiness, but it's clear she only gave up her dream for yours and mine. We were selfish in holding her with us this long."

He'd meant to reassure, but Lily heard the bitter twist in his final sentence.

She put a hand on his cheek and held it there until he turned into the caress and laid a kiss on her palm, a small thank you for her sympathy. The right answer came to her then, and her hand dropped.

"You must go there yourself. Go to Dover. Find word of Sam. Stay as long as it takes."

When he began to shake his head, she caught it between both hands. "I'll be fine here on my own, and better knowing you'll learn just what happened to my little sister. I cannot stand not knowing, nor do I think you'll rest any easier. She might be as smart as you say, but Sam has never been on her own. Even if she managed the ship, would she know to send word? She could be resting safely within the haven and we'd never know."

Henry looked as though he would argue, but Lily only firmed her gaze. "You know I'm right."

The breath went out of him on a deep sigh, and he pushed to his feet. "You are, as is usually true. I just don't want to leave you now when you are suffering under such strain."

Lily managed a smile that held against any wavers. "I have

Kate and Cook and the whole of your household to watch over me. Neither am I such an invalid as of yet to need a nursemaid."

A cough spoiled her determined statement, but though his eyes narrowed, he gave a stiff nod.

"I'll go if for no other reason than to bring back something to ease your mind. If she's there, I'll find her. If she's not, there must be some evidence of her whereabouts. I had business to conduct in Dover regardless. I'll stay as long as it takes to complete so none will question my presence then rush back here with what news I've been able to obtain."

He'd caught the fever of her possibility now, and Lily knew nothing would keep him from it, a knowledge supported as he strode half out of the room before turning back.

"I'll send Kate in to attend you while I prepare for the journey. I'll leave at first light with Stuart as my companion. Highway men will be less likely to take on two able-bodied men, and we'll get there faster astride than by carriage. If there is anything to be found, I will find it."

Lily watched him swallow the distance to the servant quarters with the full measure of his long legs, a pang burning in her heart. She hoped he would find word of Sam to bring back and comfort both of them.

If her sister had done as he supposed, though, they couldn't expect to learn anything. The only time news would come of a stowaway would be if she'd been captured. In that instance, she doubted the label attached to such news would hold any connection to how Sam snuck aboard.

Lily clung to the promise Henry had given in that rumors of a Natural would fly from tongue to tongue faster than any other even when no truth existed to support the claim.

Those with the talent to transform mechanical devices as if

by magic might be fugitives in the eyes of the law, but fascination with their knack drew folks to the vicinity as much as fear kept them wary. A single slip, and Sam would become the focus of everyone's attention with none holding her needs at the fore. Henry had to find her.

Learn more about *Life and Law* on margaretmcgaffeyfisk.com.

About the Author

 Margaret McGaffey Fisk is a story-teller who explores tales across genres and worlds. Raised in the Foreign Service where she developed a love for anthropology, she has been a data entry clerk, veterinary tech, editor, support engineer, and programmer, among other roles. She pulls on her studies and experiences to give depth to the cultures and people that form the heart of her stories. As her website is titled, she offers tales to tide you over.

She'd love to hear from you through any of the contact points or social media accounts listed on her website, or you can subscribe to one of her newsletters for release announcements, snippets, and other news:

margaretmcgaffeyfisk.com/subscribe-to-my-newsletter/

Website
MargaretMcGaffeyFisk.com

Acknowledgements

Gifts signals the end of the first volume in The Steamship Chronicles, a series I wouldn't have even begun without David Bridger's encouragement. It also signals the first complete set in my indie career, so has special significance.

David Bridger is not the only one to encourage me, though. I've had the support of my immediate and extended family as I traveled this sometimes rocky road. My husband Colin continues to be the support I need in whatever variant: editing, cover consult, titles, plotting questions, and what have you. I know I can come to him for feedback and he'll be happy to weigh in with an opinion or two. My sons have also been resources for both encouragement and specific feedback, especially when I'm wavering. Without them, from as early as the age of three on plot walks, I would not be the writer I am now.

My parents and sisters are endlessly patient as well, listening to book blurbs, editing pieces, or peering at cover art to identify where I might have slipped up. They push me to be better and to make what I put out in the world stronger.

Once again, though, it is my readers who make this journey possible. The first book I put out with a hope and a prayer. You have made me delighted to keep writing and publishing new novels for your pleasure and mine. There is nothing quite like learning someone is eagerly waiting the next in one of my series. Without your interest, who knows whether I'd have published book two, much less book three with book four already in raw form. Thank you for taking a chance on me and enjoying the experience enough to continue to walk this path at my side.

www.ingramcontent.com/pod-product-compliance
Lightning Source LLC
Chambersburg PA
CBHW020008140726
47904CB00018B/2045